ROBBIE BALLEW

Also from Robbie Ballew:

Arianna and the Spirit of the Storm
Chrysalis and the Fire of the Forge
Chass and the War of the Storm

Prologue: Moonborn

"Pretend this is the portal," the young Fae boy sitting at Ayita's feet said as he carefully balanced two sticks in the shape of a triangular doorway. She had been his caretaker for more than ten years, yet it never ceased to amaze her how he could get so completely caught up in his imagination that he would seem oblivious to the world around him. On this night, she was particularly grateful for it.

"Careful you don't make a real portal, Ualan" Ayita teased. Her wrinkled, copper-skinned hands diligently worked to fashion a cornhusk doll from the remains of the day's harvest. Her bones ached from the brisk chill of Ohio's Autumn. She had never fully understood why her dreams had lead her to move north when so many of her people had migrated west, but a knot in her stomach told her the answer may well be delivered by sunset.

Ualan sighed and rolled his eyes. "You can't get to the fairy world from America."

"I wouldn't be so sure," she winked as she tied off the

last string on the doll. "How else could so many fair folk have gotten here?"

Ualan took the doll and looked it over, tugging at its husked legs in thought. "They came on boats, just like everyone else. Like my parents did."

"I didn't come on a boat," Ayita replied. It was refreshing to have a companion so oblivious to the significance of her lineage, but she knew the truth wouldn't hide from him forever.

"Then your parents did, or someone," Ualan said, his tone matter-of-fact.

Ayita shook her head. "My family has been here for thousands of years."

"Really?" Ualan wrinkled his nose. "I thought only humans lived here before the pilgrims?"

Ayita raised her eyebrows, encouraging him toward the inevitable realization of her humanity.

Ualan studied her face.

"It's the ears," Ayita prompted. She turned her head, and Ualan leaned in for a closer look. He gently caressed the short, rounded top of her ear, then felt the long, pointed cartilage of his own.

"You're a human?" he asked with a gentle, sincere curiosity.

"Perhaps." Ayita smiled, then diverted Ualan's attention to the cornhusk doll. "What will you name your little hero?"

Ualan marched the doll up to the imaginary gateway. "This is me when I'm big enough," he answered.

"Big enough for what?"

The doll paused at the mouth of the portal, contemplating its fate. "To save Scotland," Ualan whispered.

The doll remained frozen, afraid to take another step, unsure of what it might find.

"Is that why your family came to America?" Ayita eased into the silence. "To escape Raghnall's war?"

Ualan nodded. "My father always says we'll go back. That we'll join the fight when we're ready."

Ayita folded another bunch of corn husks into a second, slightly smaller doll. "Do you think the baby will go with you?"

Ualan looked back at the house, and Ayita followed his gaze. The flickering light of the gas lamp in his parent's room was faintly visible through the gently wafting curtains as twilight settled in. Ayita had been concerned he might hear his mother's screams, so she had taken him far enough away from the house that the sound wouldn't carry.

"If the baby is a boy, I suppose he will," Ualan answered. "Father says they'll need capable soldiers."

"I see." Ayita diverted her gaze to the horizon opposite the setting sun.

Ualan followed her stare. "Is it true? About the curse?"

Ayita glanced down at the boy. She'd wondered how much of the grown-ups' conversations he'd overhead these last few weeks. "Your father insists it's an old wives' tale."

Ualan turned and met her eyes. "But what do you think?"

Nanyehi let out a sigh. "We'll find out soon enough." A slight tremor betrayed the trepidation in her voice.

Ayita knew it would be futile to hide the truth. It was growing ever more likely that Ualan would be coming face to face with the reality of the curse very soon. "I met a werewolf myself, once."

"Was it scary?" Ualan's voice carried a sympathetic softness as only a child's voice could.

Ayita laid her hands on Ualan's shoulders and locked his eyes. "Not at all," she insisted. "She was still a person, no different from you and me. All of them are."

Ualan was confused by this new revelation. "The stories say they're blood-thirsty monsters."

"Not always," Ayita assured him. "They only turn during the full moon. And even then…" She paused. The curse was well known, but the remedy was not to be shared with any colonizer. It was an antidote reserved for her people. "Ualan, there is hope yet."

"How?"

Her momentary hesitation created a heavy silence, punctured by a blood-curdling scream from the house.

"Mommy!" Ualan shouted as he scrambled toward the house.

Ayita caught him and pulled him into a relentless embrace. Ualan's tears soaked her blouse as his mother's cries drenched the gentle twilight. The tip of the full moon had crested over the edge of the Earth.

"Why?" Ualan fought against Ayita's grip. "Why would your people make such a curse?"

Ayita knew that no answer could bring him comfort. Still, she had to try. "The curse was woven into the fabric of this land long ago, when nations battled fiercely to expand their territory. That's why it only affects children born under a full moon on stolen land. They never knew all our lands would be stolen by invaders from across the sea."

Between Ualan's sobs and his mother's cries, Ayita couldn't be sure the boy had heard her.

The slam of a door startled Ayita, and Ualan broke free of her grip. He tore toward the house but stopped short upon seeing his father marching into the barn. Tension curled up from Murchadh's balled fists to his broad shoulders, sweat matting his deep black hair, and blood staining his once-white tunic.

He soon returned—knuckles white as they gripped an axe. Ualan gasped.

"Murchadh, don't!" Ayita yelled, dashing forward to meet him.

Murchadh spun on his heel and raised the axe in Ayita's direction. "You have no right to speak here, you Vanaran bitch!" His Scottish accent was more pronounced than usual as anger permeated his voice.

Ayita snarled at the derogation. "You readily accepted me into your family, and now you—"

"My *wife* accepted you." He lowered the axe, his voice cracking on the words. "My *dead* wife. Millina always had a soft spot for you savages."

"M-mommy?" Ualan whimpered, retreating behind Ayita.

"That baby is still your son!" Ayita was searching for a crack in Murchadh's stoic facade, but he revealed no such weakness.

"He's moonborn," Murchadh spat. "He's cursed! I'll not have that stain on my family's name."

Ualan looked up at Ayita. "Moonborn?" he asked.

Ayita put a hand on Ualan's shoulder, gritted her teeth, and steeled her resolve. "It can be stopped," she said to Murchadh. It felt like a betrayal of her people to reveal such a closely guarded secret, but the overwhelming guilt for betraying Ualan ripped it from her lips. "When a werewolf is born, there is soon after born an *Anidawehi*."

Murchadh threw his arms in the air. "And I'm supposed to know what the fuck that is?"

"You might call it an Angel. As long as they touch during the full moon, he won't turn."

Murchadh snarled, spittle flying from his mouth. "You're telling me there is some Vanaran baby out there who can make my son pretend to be normal? Am I supposed to be Herod, rounding up all the infants to find them?"

"There is a group among my kind," Ayita shouted over him, "Angel Hunters. They can find your son's partner."

Murchadh spun the axe in his hand, furious eyes flickering between Ualan and Ayita. "And I'm meant to raise a feral babe and a weak-willed son on my own?

Ualan winced. "Father—"

Murchadh threw the axe on the ground. "If you can fix the mutt, why don't you raise it yourself?" He turned toward the stable.

Ayita recognized the absolute resignation that twisted his face. Ualan's father was leaving all of this behind.

"Murchadh," Ayita pleaded, "you can't just abandon—"

"Ualan!" Murchadh beckoned as he faded into a silhouette in the hazy, purple dusk. "You've five seconds to join me, boy."

Ualan stood frozen, clenching Ayita's apron.

"B-but, my brother," Ualan murmured. "I-I can't—"

Murchadh led his horse into the yard. "Useless runt. Moving to this fucking hellscape was a mistake," he lamented, then continued his egress. He mounted the horse and snapped its reins, his form fading into the night.

Ayita clenched a hand over Ualan's ear, but it was far

too late to shield him from his new reality. "Let's get you in the house," she whispered.

Ayita settled him on the couch and steeled herself before entering Millina's room. The familiar metallic smell of blood assaulted her as soon as she crossed the threshold. The doctor, a well-regarded Faun, sat at the bedside. He was collecting his tools into a bag. He appeared deaf to the snarling and scratching sounds emanating from a small cage in the corner of the room. The once pristine, white sheets covered the late lady's head. Blood drenched the foot of the bed.

"You'll have to give the boy a name," the doctor said, peering above his spectacles at Ayita.

"Doctor, how—" Ayita began, but was interrupted by the gentle creaking of the door-frame. She turned, surprised to see Ualan had followed after her. "Ualan! You shouldn't—" her words trailed. There were a lot of things that shouldn't have happened that night.

"His name?" Ualan asked. Tears streaked his cheeks, and the boy's trembling hand gripped the door handle. He set his jaw and shook his head, wearing a more mature expression than his age deemed fit.

"You don't have to do this," Ayita said, her heart shattering as she watched the last glitters of childhood fade from Ualan's eyes.

Ualan straightened his posture and declared, "Like daddy said, my brother's name is Moonborn."

❧ Chapter One ❧

A lone rider approached a sleepy town. Her hazy silhouette was visible from miles away. The unfazed locals were more than accustomed to unexpected visitors and passers-through. They went about their business as the traveler traversed the winding road, weaving her way down the gentle slopes blanketed with knee-high brush that stretched to the horizon in every direction.

Nanyehi was a young human with one objective: Stay alive.

As she drew closer, the wide-open, cloudless sky betrayed no signs of progress save for the lengthening shadows as the sun neared the end of its own day's journey.

"Perfect timing," Nanyehi said. She leaned forward to give her tired horse a reassuring pat on the neck. Her slick, black braid slipped over her shoulder and dangled in front of the red bandanna wrapped tightly around her arm, now crusty with dried blood. "What say you, Yona? Think this town will have a bounty hunter?"

The horse nickered his response. Most of these one-well towns were full of wannabe bounty hunters who assumed every stranger was a wanted outlaw. They were a Texas specialty.

Nanyehi laughed under her breath. "Will they let us stay for more than a few hours? That's the real question." She rubbed the spot on her arm, still sore from the previous night's adventure.

It had all started nearly a week earlier, when a slick-talking mayor had hired her to help deal with a werewolf problem. She followed a few bogus leads from the sheriff until the full moon revealed it was the sheriff himself who was the werewolf. He gave her a nice scratch on the arm, and in return she'd given him a silver bullet to the heart. She'd retrieved the spent round—which now rested safely in her saddle bag until she needed it—then hopped on her horse and not stopped riding since. She knew she needed to skip town before the locals found their dead sheriff with his heart halfway pulled out of his chest, and his apparently deranged murderer still on the loose. By now there were likely wanted posters on their way to every town in a hundred mile radius.

Yona sauntered down the main strip, and Nanyehi scoffed at the ramshackle wood structures that passed for buildings. The weathered beams holding up canted porches were worn smooth by more than a few sandstorms. She hoped it wouldn't take long to find the saloon—if this speck of dust on a map even had one. The orange light piercing down the westward-facing street painted the clouds of dust kicked up by her horse's heavy steps.

A pair of suspicious eyes leered from beside a post

where their owner, a Chupacabra, was leaning. His long snout twitched as his lips curled up to reveal razor-sharp fangs. His ears protruded through holes in a dusty straw hat and angled attentively in the rider's direction. Spindly, grey-furred fingers hovered meaningfully by his belt.

Nanyehi tipped her hat with a gentle smile that feigned nothing to hide. She brushed back the tail of her leather coat to reveal a well-used revolver. She unholstered it and gave it a spin. "The new eighteen-fifty-one navy model," she said. "You seen it yet? That Colt fellow outdid himself this time."

The Chupacabra shifted his hand to the cigar in his mouth and gripped it with his palm facing outward—a subtle sign of surrender.

Nanyehi returned her gun to its hiding place and gave him a short salute—a reciprocation that neither of them was worth the other's time. "Is there a watering hole in this town?"

"Just the one." He blew a ring of smoke into the sky and gestured over his shoulder. His eyes lingered curiously on Nanyehi. "Not much work around these parts lately."

"Only looking for a drink, friend," Nanyehi replied, plying Yona's sides with her heels. "Thanks for the help."

"Mhm." He took another puff from his cigar and re-laxed against the post. Nanyehi knew as soon as she was out of sight he would head straight for the nearest bulletin board to check if any of the posters had her face on them. It would only be a matter of time before one of them did.

The saloon was easy enough to find; it was the tallest building in town. With any luck, it still had a room to spare. Nanyehi found the hitching post and tied Yona's reins in a slipped buntline hitch. To the casual onlooker, the horse was well secured. If Yona pulled hard enough, it would release—perfect for a quick getaway if things turned ugly.

She passed through the swinging half-doors and scanned the near-empty room: a ragtag bunch played poker at a round table while a few loners brooded in dark corners. Nanyehi's entrance earned her a lazy gaze and a grunt, but the card table seemed far more interested in their hands.

One particular loner seemed especially interested in the newcomer. Their eye's met, and Nanyehi's heart skipped a beat. He was attractive, to be sure—his muscular arms and sun-soaked skin gave Nanyehi visions of a pioneer hoisting bales of hay amidst a field of golden wheat swaying in the breeze—but it was more than that. A voice in the back of her head told she had been fated to come here; fated to meet this man.

She shook her head clear of the fantasy. She didn't believe in fate.

Nanyehi had barely taken her seat at the bar before Farm Boy was at her side.

"Buy you a drink?" Farm Boy asked.

Nanyehi cocked an eyebrow. He was either bold or stupid. Either way, this was going to be fun.

She took note of his pointed ears. "Fae, is it? Let me guess, Scandinavian?"

"Scottish, actually," he answered. "Ualan's the name."

Ualan appeared to be a few years younger than Nanyehi. Given the varying lifespans of different races, it was difficult to judge. His dark, thick hair and trimmed beard looked clean enough. She couldn't deny he was handsome, but it would take a lot more than a stiff jawline to impress her. She had been scammed more than once by someone who had put up a facade of congeniality. Perhaps she would get a chance to out-con a crook at his own game.

"Ualan?" Nanyehi repeated out of politeness. She had no intention of committing the name to memory. "Nanyehi," she offered in return.

"Nanyehi," Ualan said. It was no small feat that he pronounced it correctly on the first try. "Don't see many humans out in these parts."

Nanyehi noted the significance with which he used the word 'human.' She had grown so accustomed to being called 'Vanaran' that she almost expected it. She never understood how it had become standard to refer to humans as Vanaran, who in actuality were a race of monkey-like people from halfway across the world. Four hundred years earlier, one Spanish idiot had thought he'd landed in India, couldn't tell the difference between one indigenous race and the other, and in all this time no one had thought to correct the misnomer.

"Nice observation," Nanyehi smirked. "But don't think it will be enough to see my human parts."

Ualan placed a hand sincerely over his heart. "Ma'am, you insult my honor. To think my intentions would be anything but—"

"Your honor?" Nanyehi interrupted him. "Is that how you wound up in a podunk town waiting to buy a drink for any woman who walks through that door?"

Ualan raised his eyebrows. "I was waiting for *you*."

Nanyehi smirked. She'd heard that one before. "Is that so?"

"I've been searching for you for years. It's fate that finally brought us together."

Fate. There was that word again. Nanyehi turned away from him, hoping to signal an end to their conversation.

"You don't even know who I am."

Ualan leaned forward and lowered his voice. "I know exactly who you are. You're a—" he paused and glanced suspiciously around the room. "I think you'd prefer I not say it out loud in such a public space."

Ah, so that was his endgame. He was trying to get her alone, wasn't he? Nanyehi nodded toward a table where a pair of locals were playing poker. "You play cards?" she asked.

"I'm familiar with the rules," Ualan answered with a humble shrug.

He was likely bluffing to paint himself as an easy target. Good. A mysterious opponent was the best kind. "One buck a buy-in," Nanyehi suggested. "You dry me out first, and I'll let you buy me that drink."

"Buy you a drink with your money?" Ualan questioned.

"Those are the rules." Nanyehi shrugged.

"I don't know, a dollar is a lot—"

"Too rich for your blood?" Nanyehi prodded. She knew she could have asked for more, but she didn't want to risk scaring him away right out of the gate. Besides, it would be easier to swindle him out of more cash once he had some blood on the table.

"It's just not what I came here for," he sighed. "I need your help."

"Oh, sweetie, if you need lessons, that's gonna cost extra," Nanyehi teased.

Ualan deflated and huffed, then leaned back in, ready to attack from a different angle. "Alright, I'll admit, it's true, I am in need of certain… 'services'. And I know for a fact that you are the only person on this continent who can give me what I want."

So he was resorting to flattery now? Nanyehi had to admit it was a good look on him. She could afford to follow this thread at least a little bit further. If it ended with the two of them in bed together, she certainly wasn't going to complain. "Then I must be worth at least one game of cards."

"Alright," he relented. "So if you win, what do you get?"

"If I win, you go back to your corner and leave me be," Nanyehi answered. Not that she wanted that to happen, but if he was going to play her game, she was sure as hell going to give him a challenge. There would be plenty of time to up the ante later. "I came here to rest, not for," she motioned between them with a wave of her hand, "whatever this is."

He furrowed his brows but nodded. "Fine. You've got a deal."

They made their way to the table and paid up. The dealer counted out their chips and dealt them into the next hand.

Nanyehi checked her cards. Pocket eights. Not the best hand she'd ever been dealt, but worth sitting out the flop for. She called. The buck came to Ualan, and he called as well. At least he wasn't one of those overly cautious players who folded until they got aces in the hole.

The dealer laid out the flop: two of diamonds, two of hearts, four of spades. That gave Nanyehi two pair. The odds that one of the other three players held a higher pocket pair than her were slim, but she didn't want to end the hand too early. She made a modest raise, and the two locals called. It was Ualan's turn to act; he matched her raise, then doubled it. Nanyehi looked back at the board.

Sure, he might have had four of a kind, but what idiot stayed in with ducks in the hole? She called; the two locals folded. They were just a distraction anyway.

Next came the turn: a six of diamonds. That wasn't helping anybody. They both checked. The river was the last card to be dealt: the eight of spades. Nanyehi couldn't believe her luck. That gave her a full house. The only hand that could beat her was that four of a kind, but she felt pretty good about her odds.

She winked at Ualan. "How's that two pair looking for you, now?"

He shifted uncomfortably, but not enough to give anything away. If he was bluffing, she would make him sweat for it.

A flurry of motion caught the corner of Nanyehi's eye as a small posse of gunslingers bustled through the swinging saloon doors. There was purpose in their strides. She spared a glance to size up the group and was glad she did; it was the Chupacabra from outside, and he was eyeing the tables like he was looking for someone. Could news of the inevitable price on her head really have caught up with her already?

"All in." She pushed her chips into the pot with enough cockiness to distract from the panic creeping in from the back of her mind.

Ualan leaned back in his chair. "All in?" he whistled. "I don't know—"

"Then why don't we spice things up a bit?" Nanyehi caught him before he had time to fold.

Ualan leaned forward. "I'm listening."

"You win, we take that drink up to your room."

"Hmm," he gave a subtle nod. "And if you win?"

"Same scenario," she shrugged, then shifted to a red-hot glare. "But I make the rules."

So much for his poker face; His wide eyes and eager grin were all the tell Nanyehi needed. Even if it was true that a wild night with her wasn't what he was after, that didn't mean it wasn't exactly what he wanted.

"All in," Ualan said as he pushed his chips in. He flipped his cards to reveal a pair of tens. "So, how'd I do?" he asked.

"You had the better hand," Nanyehi answered coyly before showing her pocket eights. "Right up until the river." Ualan deflated back into his chair. Nanyehi stood and raked in the pot.

"This is going to be fun."

Chapter Two

Nanyehi took Ualan's hand and whisked the boy upstairs, hoping not to attract too much attention. Best case scenario, they looked like an eager couple turning in early for the evening. Worst case, the Chupacabra and his gang would be on their way to bust down the door.

Ualan sat on the bed as Nanyehi closed the door behind her and shut the latch. "Keep your pistol holstered, kid," she said. "You aren't getting lucky tonight."

Ualan scrambled off the creaky, dusty mattress and straightened his shirt as he stood. "I told you. That's not why I brought you here," he said with weighted seriousness.

She moved to the window. "What," she teased, "you don't want to have sex with me?"

"No, that's not—I didn't—"

She enjoyed watching him fluster but had more pressing things to worry about. There was an eave just below the window, which made a jump to the ground possible.

Nanyehi whistled for Yona. With any luck, her horse would sneak around before the ruffians noticed, and they'd be on their way into the night within minutes. Nanyehi had been looking forward to sleeping in an actual bed, but it seemed a cot in some rocky crag was the best she could hope for.

"I brought you here," Ualan insisted, "because I need your help!"

Nanyehi glanced back at him. "Whatever you need, you've got the wrong girl."

"Dammit, will you just listen to me?" Ualan was growing frustrated.

Nanyehi didn't have time for this. "Look," she said, "I don't know who you think is in charge here—"

"You're an Angel Hunter, aren't you?"

Nanyehi froze. "What?"

"I need an Angel Hunter. I need you."

"How did you—who told you...?" Nanyehi asked, perplexed.

"Please, it's my brother," Ualan begged. "He's only twelve."

"Silver bullet," Nanyehi said, then turned to the window.

"What?" It was Ualan's turn to be confused. "I don't understand."

"Do it in his sleep. It will be easier for both of you."

"No! I'm not going to...I can't!"

"You can't?"

"I won't. Please, I need you to help me find his angel."

Nanyehi was reeling. She had no idea how this outsider had learned about angels, but she had no intention of helping him find one. "It's not enough for you people to take our land, you want our children, too?"

"It's not like that!"

"What do you think it's like? The angel has to be tied off to their werewolf every full moon until one of them dies. They would give up their entire life so your brother could live his. That's not a trade we're willing to make with colonizers."

Ualan raised a hand to his mouth. "I'm sorry, I thought—"

"You thought what? They would hold hands for a few hours, and it would all be over?"

"I didn't think—"

"You didn't think at all, did you?"

"I'm trying to do what's best for my brother! That's all I care about."

"And I'm doing what's best for my people," Nanyehi said. "We don't help outsiders, period."

"Can't you make an exception?" Ualan pleaded. "Just this once?"

"Sacagawea made an exception, and look where it got her."

"Wait," Ualan shook his head in disbelief, "you're telling me Lewis and Clark…one of them was…which one?"

"It doesn't matter." Nanyehi returned to the window. "Right now, I need you to help me get the hell out of here or shut up and stay out of my way."

Ualan stepped toward her. "Those bounty hunters are after you, aren't they?"

Nanyehi turned back and met his advance, her face inches from his. "I do what I have to to survive. For someone like me, that's more than enough to earn a price on my head."

Ualan held his ground, but the softness in his eyes

showed genuine sympathy. "If it's so dangerous, why don't you quit?"

"You think I'd do this job if I had a choice?" Nanyehi shot back. "It's what I've been trained from birth to do, and thanks to money-hungry bounty hunters like our Chupacabra friend out there, I'm the only one left who knows the ritual. Either I do it, or no one does." The sound of galloping hooves caught Nanyehi's attention, and she looked down to see Yona trotting through the back alley-way. "There's my ride," she said as she stepped through the window onto the rickety, wood-shingle eave.

"Wait!" Ualan called out. "I think I have a solution to both our problems." Nanyehi paused just long enough for Ualan to reach the window and make his offer: "Help me find an angel for my brother, and I'll let you train me to take your place."

Nanyehi's head spun around in disbelief. His stern face answered her unspoken question: He was serious! "I refused to help you find even one angel, and you think I'm gonna show you the guarded, sacred rite for finding all of them?" Her horse was waiting. Any more delay and her escape would be foiled before she even reached the edge of the city. "You are as stupid as you look," she spat as she turned and dropped onto her ready horse.

She quickly but quietly weaved her way through a maze of buildings. It didn't take long to reach the edge of town. She paused and looked out. There were a solid two hundred yards of open plains before she reached her first chance at cover in the rocky hills.

Nanyehi turned back to the town and listened. No rustling footsteps, no hushed voices; the coast seemed clear. "Let's go." She spurred her horse on and galloped into the night. She was almost halfway across when the first gun-shot rang out. The bullet impacted the ground just ahead of her and kicked up enough of a dust cloud to divert her horse. Nanyehi yanked the reins to bring it back on track and dug her heel into its hindquarters as hard as she could.

A second shot fired. This time, Yona brayed and fell to the ground, tossing Nanyehi into a prickly bush.

"Dammit!" She pulled her revolver and leveled it to-ward the town to lay down cover fire, but there was no sign of the bounty hunters in the pitch-black shadows between the buildings. They had stopped firing.

In the pale, silvery moonlight, Nanyehi could just make out a cloud of dust coming her way. Had they sicced their dogs on her? No, it was the Chupacabra! Nanyehi pulled her gun around and fired.

The bounty hunter ran on all fours and jumped to the side to evade her shot without slowing its pace. A second futile bullet bounced off the ground.

Nanyehi raised her revolver into the air to clear the burst percussion cap from the chamber and quickly real-ized she wouldn't have time to level it for another shot.

The Chupacabra leaped off its hind legs to clear the final distance between them, and Nanyehi dove behind her fallen horse; the rabid attacker slammed hard into its back. The sudden change of target didn't seem to bother the Chupacabra. Jagged teeth and claws dug into the animal's side, splattering Nanyehi with blood as she scrambled back to the relative cover of the bushes. She bolted to her feet and got a shot off before she had time to properly aim; at this range, she couldn't miss. The slug hit the Chupacabra's arm and dislodged him from his equine snack. He howled in pain. That would slow him down, at least.

Three shots fired, three more in the cylinder. Nanyehi turned and ran for the hills. She glanced back at the town. It may have been a trick of the light, but she almost thought she could see the rest of the bounty hunters hiding in the shadows, their rifles at the ready. But then, why weren't they firing? Unless…

She froze in her tracks. Her worst fears were confirmed as a glint of moonlight caught the polished barrel of a rifle mounted on a rocky crag ahead of her. The Chupacabra had slowed her down just enough for the rest of his posse to make their way through the hills and cut her off. Nanyehi got off two shots in the direction of the ambush, but she knew it was a vain gesture. Even if she'd managed to take out this one attacker, there had been at least three others in the saloon and likely more waiting outside. They would all be spread out through the hills by now—a firing squad waiting for the command to perform the execution as soon as she dared to move.

Her moment of panic was interrupted by the sound of footsteps as the injured Chupacabra approached. She still had one shot left, if only she could catch sight of the vile creature before he made his finishing move.

Without warning, a bright light flooded the entire area. Nanyehi could see the Chupacabra now. He was shielding his eyes from the source of the radiance, which seemed to be directly above and slightly behind Nanyehi. She raised her revolver.

Bam!

The bounty hunter's jaw exploded, and his limp body fell hard to the dusty earth. The light faded, making the darkness of the night even more complete than it had been a moment earlier. Nanyehi felt herself lifting off the ground and looked up as the last bit of luminance faded from Ualan's face.

"You!" Nanyehi exclaimed. "What are you—"

"I'm getting you out of here!" Ualan said as he hoisted her into the air. They were making their escape; not through the hills, but over them!

"Put me down!" Nanyehi struggled against Ualan's grip, though she couldn't be sure how high they had flown. If she managed to break free, she would likely fall to her death.

"And let those bounty hunters take you in cold?" he yelled over the howling wind as they flew into the night. "You just told me you're the only person left who can find my brother's angel," Ualan tightened his grip. "So, the only thing we have to do is keep you alive!"

Nanyehi fell silent as her new reality settled in. As much as she hated the idea of helping Ualan find an angel, he had just saved her life.

For that, she owed him.

Chapter Three

Nanyehi jerked awake. She was in a tent, alone. It was daylight outside, though what time of day she couldn't be sure. She must have fallen asleep as they were flying. It hadn't been comfortable—dangling a hundred feet above the ground in a scrawny fairy's arms—but she had been beyond exhausted. The quiet rhythms of the star-lit landscape passing beneath her feet had been accentuated by a colorful, pulsating glow, likely a result of Ualan's magical flight. The combined effect had lulled her into a dream. How long had Ualan carried her, anyway?

Memories from the night before flashed in her mind like gunshots in the dark of night. Her horse's body on the ground; the Chupacabra's mutilated face; the smoking gun in her hand. She shook her head to clear the images away. She couldn't afford to slow down, not with those bounty hunters tracking her down. She rolled over and pushed herself up to her hands and knees and felt the all-too-familiar discomfort of having slept fully clothed—boots and all. She was grateful Ualan had the decency not to take advantage of her while she was unconscious, though she wouldn't have minded at least a little effort to make her more comfortable. She couldn't complain too much. He had put up a tent and managed to drag her dead weight inside it.

She pushed her way out into the midday sun and shielded her eyes. Ualan was sitting by a fire, spit-roasting a slab of salted meat. So, he was a farm boy after all; where else could he have procured such a carefully preserved meal? Nanyehi could almost imagine him slipping into the smokehouse at his family's homestead under cover of dark and carefully selecting some choice cuts for the road. Either that, or he'd swiped the meat from the saloon's stores, but he didn't strike Nanyehi as the kind who could pull that off. He stood and faced her, his hands clenched awkwardly at his side. Whoever he was, he was a nervous wreck.

"I saved you some lunch," he said. "It's pork from my family's farm; if you like that sort of thing." He seemed a little too worried about hurting her feelings.

"I can eat and walk," she muttered.

"Where do you plan on going?" Ualan asked.

"Further away from those no-good—"

"If they could track us, which they can't, they couldn't cover that distance in less than three days," he countered.

Nanyehi spun around to face him. She knew better than to let herself feel safe. "And they'll be hot on our trail as soon as—"

"I flew us sixty miles over hills, lakes, and woods."

Nanyehi deflated. Had they traveled that far in a single night? "I'd still feel better if we kept moving," she said.

"Trust me," Ualan insisted. "You won't be hearing from those scoundrels again."

Nanyehi chuckled. "Scoundrels? Sounds like you've been reading a few too many penny dreadfuls."

"I was… doing my research," Ualan fumbled.

Nanyehi wasn't sure if his naivete was charming or downright terrifying. She'd have to work twice as hard to watch their backs. She sat next to the fire and pulled the meat off the spit. "So, then, now what?" she asked.

Ualan rubbed his hands together. "I hoped you would help me find my brother's angel."

"Do you think I can just say a few magic words and tell you where to find your precious angel?" She was stalling. Sure, she owed him her life, but could she really betray the secret of her people to this colonizer? It was so much bigger than just her life. She would just have to lead him on until she found her chance to break free.

Ualan pursed his lips. "I understand the spell is more complicated than that," he said.

An awkward silence fell between them. Nanyehi picked away a strip of meat and chewed it. "How did you know? About me?"

"My caretaker. Ayita. She raised us after my father left. The day Moon…" he cut himself off and shook his head. "The day my brother was born."

"Ah." He didn't have to tell Nanyehi what happened to his mother. She'd seen this many times before. "Ayita? That's a Cherokee name."

"She'd only heard stories about you. Finding you was… difficult." Ualan ran a hand through his hair.

"I guess so." Nanyehi chewed through another piece of pork. Curiosity got the better of her. "Did Ayita tell you about the ingredients I need?"

Ualan pulled a pouch from his belt. "A tuft of fur from the, uh, the turned?" he asked, handing her the satchel.

Nanyehi narrowed her eyes at the pouch but didn't bother taking it from his hands to check the contents. Had another human willingly trusted Ualan enough to betray the secret of their people and send him to Nanyehi? She had an easier time believing he had garnered that information through more nefarious means.

"I understand there are more items we'll need to gather." Ualan pulled her from her reverie.

"Hmm?"

"The other ingredients for the spell. What are they, and how do we find them?"

"Oh. Right." Nanyehi sighed. There was no point lying about it. She would need all the ingredients for the next time she performed the ritual, even if it wasn't going to be for Ualan's brother. "We need a piece of silver."

"That's not so—"

"That's been used to kill a werewolf," she finished.

"I see."

"Yeah," Nanyehi muttered as she stood and paced. She had a few leads to go on, she just had to think which one would be closest... "You got a map?" She spun on her heel.

"You travel without a map?" He reached for his bag.

"My things went down with Yona." He tilted his head in confusion. She added, "My horse."

"Right. Sorry," he pulled out a handful of carefully folded papers. "Just Texas, or—"

"No, the whole U.S. if you have it," Nanyehi held out her hand. "Actually both. I need to figure out where we are before I know where we're headed."

Ualan found the right pages and helped her lay them out on the ground. Nanyehi immediately noticed they were covered in marks and scribbled notes. She looked up at Ualan. He shrugged.

"I spent a long time looking for you," he said.

Nanyehi found a tiny dot on the Texas map. "Last night we were here. Which way did we fly?" she asked.

"North-east-ish, I think," Ualan looked over her shoulder at the map.

"Great, so that puts us somewhere around…" she traced a path away from the tiny dot.

"Here," Ualan pointed out a spot in the middle of nowhere. "I think I recognize that lake." For most people, seeing the lake in person would have looked nothing like it did on the map. That's because most people would be looking at it from the ground. Ualan, Nanyehi realized, got to see the world from a bird's-eye view.

Nanyehi found the same area on the larger map. "That puts us about a week's ride from Nashville if we could find some horses."

"I'm not flying us that far if that's what you're thinking," Ualan said.

Nanyehi shot him a sideways glance.

He put his hands up defensively. "Magic is like a muscle; overuse it and it gets sore and tired. It'll be a few days before I can pull another stunt like that."

"Hmm," Nanyehi hummed a noncommittal noise, then turned back to the map of Texas. "We might be in luck. There's a railway not ten miles north of here."

Ualan studied the map over her shoulder. "How far to the station? I should have enough left to buy—"

"You've never had to travel with a human before, have you? They don't exactly let us sit in first class."

"They wouldn't have to know who the ticket was for, would they?"

"Trust me, kid, I don't wanna get thrown in with the livestock again. I say save your money; let's hop an empty box car."

"Hop an empty box car?"

"What, you've never hopped a train before?"

"I can't say that I've ever needed to."

"And that's why you'll never have what it takes to be an angel hunter. Your life has been too easy."

"Easy? You think running a farm at twelve years old is easy?"

Nanyehi grabbed Ualan's arm and squeezed. "Oh sure, you've got those big farm-boy muscles from slinging hay and manure all day, but you don't have the instincts to survive in the real world. I have to make a hundred split-second decisions every single day, knowing that even one tiny mistake could be my last."

Ualan pulled free from her grip and moved to sit back down by the fire. "We'll leave first thing in the morning."

"And what do you propose we do until then?" Nanyehi asked. "Sing campfire songs? We can reach it by nightfall if we pack up now."

"What's the rush?" Ualan asked. "I told you we're safe here."

"Safe's got nothing to do with it," Nanyehi answered as she folded the map. "I just don't like sitting still when I've got someplace to go." She headed to her tent to tear it down.

"Fine, have it your way." Ualan set to work putting out

the fire. "So, what's in Nashville?"

"About seventy miles south of it, actually," Nanyehi clarified. "You remember what I told you about Sacagawea?"

"She was an angel, right? So, which one was the werewolf? Lewis or Clark?"

"Well, William Clark lived to the ripe old age of sixty-eight, but Meriwether Lewis—"

"That's right," Ualan remembered. "He was shot while staying at an inn on the Natchez Trace. I always heard it was suicide."

Nanyehi paused her work and looked over at him. "If you were going to commit suicide, would you shoot yourself in the head *and* the stomach?"

"Huh. No, I suppose I wouldn't," Ualan answered. "You think the bullets are still there?"

"It's a long shot, I'll admit," she said. "But our other option is we hunt down and kill a werewolf. Are you ready to kill a werewolf, Ualan?"

Ualan frowned. "Not if we can avoid it."

Nanyehi nodded. "The feeling's mutual."

Chapter Four

Twilight settled over the barren Texas landscape as the long, slithering train track came into view. A handful of wispy, pink clouds textured the vast, wide-open sky.

Ualan settled down behind a rocky crag, just out of view of any oncoming trains. "Now we wait."

"Now we plan. Give me your map of Tennessee."

"You never stop, do you?" Ualan slid his pack off his shoulder and rummaged through it.

"Once we get the silver bullet—"

Ualan plopped a folded paper on the ground in front of Nanyehi. "*If* we get the silver bullet."

"Whether we do or don't, we'll need horses." Nanyehi quickly opened the map. "There's not a lot of overlap between places humans live and where trains run."

"Alright, so where do we get horses?"

Nanyehi ran a finger along the train route. "Here's the inn… If we head north from there we should hit a farm just outside of Nashville."

"A farm?" Ualan scoffed. "Or a plantation?"

Nanyehi cocked an eyebrow. She was taken aback by the sudden disdain in Ualan's voice. "What's the difference?"

"In Ohio, we have farms. In the south—"

"Ah, so you don't own slaves. Congratulations. You shouldn't have any qualms stealing a couple of horses from a slave owner, then."

"I'm more worried about what he'll do to his slaves when he finds a few horses missing."

"You can't save everyone."

Ualan shook his head. "I've always been taught to never—"

"*I* was taught to do whatever it takes to get the job done," Nanyehi cut in, "and that's what I'm going to do."

"—to never refuse help to a being in need," Ualan finished. "Certainly not to make things worse for them."

"Really? Where'd you learn that? From a—"

"From a human."

Nanyehi pursed her lips.

"Ayita was there for my brother and me when we needed her most. She didn't care that our ears were different shapes. She didn't care about how my father had treated her. She took us in and raised us as if we were her own. To be honest, some days I feel more Human than Fae."

Nanyehi huffed and forced herself to continue studying the map. "Most days I feel like I'd rather be anything *but* Human. Doesn't make it true, does it?"

Nanyehi could feel Ualan's eyes bear down on the top of her head. She refused to look up and meet his gaze. She didn't need his pity. A distant whistle gave her the out she needed. She hastily folded the map and shoved it into

Ualan's arms. "Let's get ready. About three-quarters of the way back, we should find an open box car."

"And if we don't find one with an open door?"

"Then we'd better hope they don't have locks."

Ualan perked up and halfway reached for his bag as if he had just remembered something. "I might have something to help with that."

Nanyehi cocked an eyebrow and shot Ualan a dubious side-eye. She didn't even want to ask. In any case, she was certain that his idea of what would be helpful in this situation was entirely different from hers.

They watched and waited for several tense moments. With each passing car, the knot in Nanyehi's stomach grew tighter. Not a single door was open.

Ualan shifted uneasily behind her. "Let's just make a run for it. Trust me, I've got this."

"I don't trust you," Nanyehi said through gritted teeth. That didn't change the fact they didn't have a choice. She bolted full speed toward the train. She could hear Ualan's footsteps following close behind her, but they were soon drowned out by the rhythmic clanking of metal.

Her path intersected the train's just in time to catch the tail end of a passing car. She deftly leaped, took hold of the corner, and perched herself on the rear coupling. She scooted toward the edge and reached around far enough to grab the closed sliding door. She gave it a solid pull, but it refused to budge.

"Fuck!" she yelled.

She peered into the darkness behind her. With any luck, Ualan had missed the train completely. She couldn't make out any sign of him on the other train cars or the ground. Her momentary relief was short-lived as a glint of multi-colored light caught the corner of her eye. She spun around to see Ualan flying alongside the train holding what appeared to be a large pair of cutting pliers. Did he think he was strong enough to cut through a solid steel lock?

Ualan raised the pliers to the lock and almost seemed to struggle to pull them open. He placed the teeth around the bolt and in one clean *snap!* it broke loose!

Nanyehi pulled back just in time as the heavy sliding door flew open and nearly knocked her from her perch. The flying wall of metal reached the end of its track with a loud *clang!* then bounced back toward its starting point. Once it had sufficiently settled down, Nanyehi climbed onto it and expertly kept her grip even as it slid back and forth with the unpredictable motion of the train. She carefully made her way toward the opening, and just as she was about to swing around into the box car, Ualan's hand reached out to take hold of hers. Without thinking, she swatted it away and yelled, "I don't need your help!"

It was a careless move. Before she had time to re-establish her grip, the train hit a bump. Her feet slipped, and the hand that had been inches away from grabbing the side of the door now swiped through thin air. Her other hand still held fast to the top of the door, but the impact of her full body weight suddenly pulling against her arm broke its grip immediately.

Her mind flashed back to the first—and last—time she had fallen off a train. She had broken several bones, and been forced to walk miles back to town with her leg in a hobbled-together splint.

She braced for the impact, but before it came a hand grabbed her wrist and swung her around. She regained her bearings just in time to see the rapidly approaching box car floor. She managed to get her feet under her and land at a full run. Ualan let go of her arm, and her momentum carried into the back of the car. She raised her arms and caught herself against the metal wall just before slamming full-force into it. It wasn't her most graceful landing, but she was grateful Ualan had the good sense not to pull into some heroic embrace like the characters in those books of his no doubt would have. It certainly would not have worked out as well for him as it always did for his fictional role models.

He also had the good sense not to say anything as she stood frozen for several minutes, catching her breath and settling her racing heart. "Those cutters," she turned and asked when she was ready, "how did you manage to break the lock?"

"Oh, these?" Ualan picked up the tool from the floor. "I added a spring here between the handles," he pointed as he handed them to Nanyehi. "They're hard as hell to pull open, but once that tension snaps them back together, they'll cut through just about anything."

Nanyehi gave them a quick test pull and found that she could hardly get them to budge without significantly more force than she felt compelled to exert at that moment. She tossed them toward Ualan's bag on the floor. "You made them yourself?"

Ualan shrugged as he picked up the pliers and looked them over. "I suppose I do quite a bit of tinkering. I'm always thinking of ways to make things work better."

Nanyehi smirked and cocked an eyebrow. "And you decided to bring them along... why? To show off your cute invention?"

Ualan's faint smile disappeared, and he quickly buried

his creation deep in his pack. "I don't know, I just had a feeling they might come in handy." He turned and locked eyes with Nanyehi. "I guess you could say I trusted my instincts."

Nanyehi huffed. "You get first watch. Wake me up in four hours." She turned away from him and settled as comfortably as she could into the far corner of the train car.

"Why keep a watch?" Ualan asked. "Shouldn't we both get as much rest as we can?"

Nanyehi rolled over toward him. "I'm sorry, did your instincts forget to tell you about the bandits that lay in wait along train routes to ambush unsuspecting travelers?" Even in the dim moonlight, Nanyehi could see Ualan's doubtful expression. "Where do you think all those dents came from?"

Ualan's eyes darted between the various bullet-sized hills that dotted the landscape of the smooth, metal walls. He surreptitiously slid out of view of the train car's open door. "Fine," he huffed. "But first... can we talk?"

"No." Nanyehi rolled onto her side, her back to Ualan.

"It's just... it's about the bounty hunters."

Nanyehi quickly flipped and propped herself up on an elbow. "What about them?" she prompted.

"I've been meaning to say..." Ualan shifted positions, turning away from Nanyehi. She guessed he was about to shift the direction of the conversation, as well. "...I mean, it seems like someone in your line of work would want to keep a low profile. So why were the bounty hunters after you?"

Nanyehi plopped down onto her back. She was certain that wasn't what Ualan had originally planned to say. No matter, she had no doubt she would be able to coax the truth out of him when the time was right. "My job is more than just finding angels for Human werewolves. I also protect them from werewolf hunters."

"What about non-human werewolves?"

"When I find one, I become the hunter."

❧ **Chapter Five** ❧

The two travelers silently approached the inn as the sun hovered just over the treetops of the heavily forested Tennessee hills. It was going to be a full moon that night, Nanyehi knew. She glanced over at Ualan. His pensive stare confirmed that he also understood the night's significance. He was no doubt thinking about his brother, who was likely being chained down and locked away at that very moment. As they passed by a cabin on the outskirts of the grounds, there was no mistaking the determination on his face. He was willing to do whatever it took to save his brother.

They approached the central building of the compound and paused. From the outside looking in, the place seemed abandoned. Nanyehi pushed open the front door, and the gentle bell announced their arrival. They emerged into a small dining area with a reception desk to one side.

A handful of roughshod travelers sat around the table finishing their evening meal. The sound of clanking silverware came to an abrupt halt as the diners turned to take in the newcomers.

"Hi," Ualan took a hesitant step forward, projecting an air of geniality.

Nanyehi cringed at his saccharin smile but knew her abrasive personality wasn't suited to making friends. Since they needed to avoid any suspicions from these strangers, she bit her tongue.

Ualan continued, "We were hoping to find a place to stay for the night."

The group exchanged uncomfortable glances. An especially gruff-looking patron—a satyr with stout, ridged horns and tufts of fur protruding from the unbuttoned cuffs of his sleeves—turned back to Ualan. "You'll need to be talking to Halfy," he said in a throaty growl. "I'm afraid he's turned in for the night."

"Halfy?" Nanyehi couldn't suppress a chuckle. She had been wondering about the seat at the head of the table, which seemed to be built up like an infant's highchair, but with a tiny ladder climbing up the side. "What is he, a gnome?"

"Coblynau, actually," a thin voice said from somewhere behind the reception desk. They turned just in time to see a wisp of gray hair rise above the countertop, followed by a kind, wrinkly face—presumably Halfy's—climbing onto a stool to greet them.

The table grew noticeably more tense, though the guests did their best to hide their apprehension—a sharp intake of breath here, a grip tightening around silverware there.

The Satyr half stood from his seat. "Halfy, shouldn't you be…" he paused and shot a quick sideways glance at the visitors.

"In bed?" Halfy finished the question. "It's still early yet," he waved dismissively, then turned to address Nanyehi and Ualan.

"Everything all right, sir?" Ualan asked.

"My regular guests are very concerned about my health, you see. I'll admit: at my age one can't deny the importance of a good night's rest!"

His age? Nanyehi wouldn't have been surprised to learn he was over one hundred years old, or at least very near it.

"We don't mean to keep you." Ualan glanced at the patrons around the table. "Is there anyone else who can help us?"

"No," Halfy chuckled, "I'm the only one who does any work around here. Hard to keep good help at a haunted inn."

"Haunted?" Nanyehi asked as she and Ualan exchanged surprised glances.

"Aye," Halfy answered. "There's been all sorts of unexplained shenanigans reported around that cabin at the top of the hill."

Nanyehi grabbed Ualan's arm. "We'll take it!" she said.

Halfy's eyes grew almost as wide as Ualan's.

"Really?" Halfy asked.

Nanyehi gave Ualan a sideways glance, "We're always looking for a little more excitement in our relationship."

Ualan was taken aback by her sudden feigned eagerness, but quickly regained his composure and played the part. "Ah, yes, that does sound like exactly what we've been looking for."

"I see," Halfy smirked. "Unfortunately, it's been locked up tight since even before I took over the place."

"We could take a look around that cabin if you like?" Nanyehi pressed. "My beau has a special touch with the paranormal."

"Well, best I can do—" he turned around and balanced precariously on the edge of the stool to reach a key hanging on the wall behind him, "—is the next closest cabin down the hill. It'll be the one you passed on your way in."

"Yes. We saw it," Nanyehi sighed as she accepted the key. "Are you certain we can't just take a peek at that cabin?"

Halfy's smile widened. "I would caution such a fine couple away from it." He lowered his voice and leaned in close. "But I hear they get a little wild at night."

Nanyehi nodded. *Perfect.* "How much do we owe you?"

"Tell you what," Halfy said. "First night's free for the love birds. Just knowing you're enjoying my hospitality is payment enough for me." He shot a quick wink in the direction of the Satyr, who—Nanyehi could just see in the corner of her eye—gave a grim smile before finally relaxing and returning to his meal. These people were hiding something. Hopefully, that was a good sign that they were on the fast track to silver. "I trust you can find your way?"

Nanyehi snapped back to the moment. "Oh, right, yes, of course, we don't want to keep you."

"Good, good," Halfy waved them toward the door. "Breakfast will be served first thing in the morning. That is if you aren't otherwise occupied." He winked at Ualan.

Ualan gave a coy shrug as Nanyehi pulled him toward the door. "Who knows what the night may bring?"

"Who knows, indeed?" Halfy half-mumbled as the two travelers exited the inn.

Safely outside, Ualan whispered, "Why did everyone look ready to jump out of their skin?"

"I don't know, but I'm guessing it won't be long before we find out."

There was just enough of dusky twilight to guide them up the path to the cabin. The key struggled to find its way into the rusty lock, and Nanyehi shouldered the long-disused door to force it free of the frame. It finally gave and opened into a rustic one-room dwelling full of dust and shadows.

Ualan went to light an oil lamp on a side table, but Nanyehi raised a hand to stop him. "Best to let our eyes adjust to the night," she said.

"Huh," Ualan was impressed. "I'd never thought of that."

"Lesson one," Nanyehi said. "You're gonna have to start thinking about things."

Ualan scoffed as he sat on the edge of the bed, which took up most of the room. "I think about things." After a moment's pause, he turned back toward Nanyehi. "Wait, what do you mean, 'lesson one'?"

"Our deal at the saloon?" Nanyehi reminded him. "You said you wanted me to train you."

"Train me to...?" Ualan must have remembered what she was talking about, Nanyehi guessed he was just fishing for confirmation.

"To be an angel hunter," Nanyehi answered. She had no intention of actually training him, but she had a hunch this was the best way to get his guard down. If she lulled him to sleep, she could sneak of to find the silver bullet and be halfway to who-knows-where before he ever realized he'd been abandoned.

Ualan cocked an eyebrow. "You made it pretty clear there was no way in hell you'd take that deal."

"That was before I was stuck owing you a life debt." Nanyehi stepped closer to Ualan, stopping inches before his face. He smelled like sweat and the dusty roads. Getting him to sleep would be easier if she wore him out a little, first. "Speaking of deals, I believe you still owe me a night on my terms."

"Wait, Nanyehi, you don't have to—"

"I want to." She put her hands on his shoulders, guiding him to lie back on the bed.

"I didn't think you were interested," Ualan murmured.

"You're not the only one surprised." She whispered into his ear, nibbling on the lobe. He shivered beneath her touch. "Do you want me to stop?" Sliding her hands down his chest, she repositioned her hips on his thighs and reached for his belt buckle.

"No, but I… I mean, is this the best time?"

The bulge in his pants betrayed him. She traced her fingers along the length of his shaft. "I think we deserve a break, don't you?"

Ualan's breath caught in his throat, and he bunched the blankets into his palms.

"We need to wait till everyone is asleep before we can take a look around," Nanyehi murmured. "Besides, I have no doubt they'll come snooping to check we are who we say we are. Might as well make it convincing, right?"

"All right," Ualan conceded. He stroked her hair, letting his fingers trail down the side of her face.

"Just relax, and I'll do the work." Nanyehi yanked down his pants and set him free. She stroked his full length; an involuntary moan was the only answer he could muster. His body produced a gentle, pulsating glow as each wave of pleasure washed over him.

"We should have done this sooner," she said as her body lulled itself into slow, rhythmic movements, and idle thoughts fell by the wayside in the back of her mind. "If only those bounty hunters hadn't been right outside our door at the saloon…"

Her hand stopped mid-stroke, a realization bursting through to the surface. "They were right outside our door," Nanyehi repeated.

"What's wrong?" Ualan propped himself up on his elbows.

"One minute they were outside our door," Nanyehi's grip tightened as pieces moved into place. "The next they were cutting off my escape."

"A-ah!" Ualan reflexively reached down to relieve the pressure but knew there was nothing he could do. He was caught in her snare.

"How could they have gotten ahead of me so fast," Nanyehi mused, "unless they knew where I was going?" She was no longer aware of how tightly she was squeezing.

"W-wait, I was going to tell you," Ualan eked out.

"You were going to tell me what?" Nanyehi stood and released her grip.

Ualan quickly scrambled to pull his pants up and fasten his belt.

"You tipped them off, didn't you?" Nanyehi demanded.

"I just thought—"

"Clearly, you didn't," Nanyehi spat.

"I thought I could convince you to help me if I—"

"If you what? Swooped in and saved the poor helpless damsel in distress?"

Ualan rose to his feet. He regained his composure and matched Nanyehi's intensity with his own. "Look, you said you do what you have to to survive. Well, I'm willing to do whatever it takes to save my brother."

"Including betting with other people's lives?"

"I took a risk, yes, but I had no other choice."

"That's the problem with gambling. Eventually, you lose."

Nanyehi turned and stormed out into the moonlit night before Ualan had a chance to say anything else. It wasn't as clean a break as she had been hoping for, but at least it was a break.

She took a deep breath of cool, crisp air, and felt the fog clearing from her senses. So Ualan had manipulated her into helping him. Could she really blame him? She would have done the same in his shoes. If she was being honest with herself, she had to admit it wasn't the sting of betrayal that hurt so much as the knowledge she had been outsmarted. Perhaps Ualan did have what it took to be an angel hunter, after all.

None of that mattered anymore. Nanyehi was once again on her own, and she would have to find a way forward—alone. That way forward started with finding the silver bullet that had killed Meriwether Lewis.

She set off up the hill, careful not to make a sound as she traversed the dense underbrush. If she was right about the satyr's intent to keep an eye on her and Ualan, it would be almost impossible to keep him from tracking her—satyrs were notoriously good trackers—but she had to try. Time almost seemed to stand still as she painstakingly charted a path from tree to tree.

A distant noise caught her attention, and she froze to listen. She slowed her breath to quiet her heart as it pounded in her chest. She singled out every sound she could identify: the chirping of crickets, the croaking of frogs, nothing out of the ordinary. No sign of hunters on her trail.

Her eyes came back into focus, and she discovered she had been staring right at a slug as it made its way around the trunk of a nearby tree, its silvery trail shimmering in the light of the full moon. It hadn't been there before, had it? She must have paused to listen much longer than she'd realized. She continued on her way, and by the time she came to the edge of the clearing where the cabin sat nestled atop the hill, the full moon hung high overhead. She made her way around the perimeter, checking each tree for any sign of a lodged bullet. It would be long overgrown and deep in the heart of the tree by now, but the gnarled knot that would have formed around it ought to have been visible.

Her heart nearly leaped out of her chest when a glint of metal caught the corner of her eye. It couldn't be that easy, could it? As she drew closer, she discovered the object wasn't a bullet, but a gun! And an antique at that, a turn-of-the-century model if her assessment was correct. A little closer and she could see the gun was held by a hand—not one of flesh, but of bone! She rounded the tree from which it was suspended to find a mangled mess of bones strung together by bits of decaying flesh. The remainder of the skeleton had fallen into a scattered pile at the base of the tree.

"What the fuck?" she whispered before she could stop herself. It was no wonder this place had earned a reputation for being haunted. Could this have been the body of Meriwether Lewis himself, morbidly commemorating the spot where the werewolf was slain? No, she thought, this body was much too tall. Lewis, she remembered from a portrait, had been much smaller. Almost like a—she caught her breath and stumbled backward as realization hit her—like a gnome.

Another glint of metal turned her attention to a second decaying body, this one holding a knife. There was no mistaking it: the blade was pure silver. Two more corpses came into focus behind the second one, each holding its own silver weapon. One was still fresh enough to reveal the distinctive wounds of a werewolf attack, though the claw marks were much smaller than Nanyehi had seen before. These were werewolf hunters who had failed in their mission. They were trophies marking the victories of the Coblynau werewolf, Meriwether Lewis.

The sound of a scuffle pulled Nanyehi back to reality. She spun around to see the satyr dragging a bound and gagged Ualan toward the cabin.

"Halfy," the satyr called in a sing-song voice. "Dinner's here!"

He pulled a key from his belt with his free hand and unlocked the cabin door. As quickly as he could, he pulled the door open, threw Ualan inside, and slammed the door closed behind him. Before he had a chance to turn the key and lock the door, Nanyehi ripped the silver knife from the fallen hunter's hand and charged out of the woods. Her free hand instinctively released her pistol from its holster. The satyr reached for his gun when he caught sight of her, but it was too late; Nanyehi had beaten him to the draw. She paused her advance long enough to take careful aim and shot him straight through the heart. It was the only sure way to get a clean kill on such a formidable creature.

Before his body hit the ground, Nanyehi was at the

door. She threw it open and stormed inside. It was almost pitch black, but in a thin sliver of moonlight, Nanyehi could make out Ualan sprawled out on his back, helplessly kicking at the attacking werewolf. The minuscule beast snapped at Ualan's ankles like a small dog. Nanyehi knew better than to underestimate its ferociousness based on its deceptive size.

The creature latched onto Ualan's leg and bit down hard. Ualan howled in pain. Nanyehi was too late. Without thinking, she flew across the room. The beast was in a frenzy. Its bloodlust kept it single-mindedly focused on the kill. It didn't even see her coming until it was pinned against a wall, a silver blade protruding from its chest. Nanyehi kept her grip tight on the handle until the creature's final breath leaked out, and its body went limp.

She looked down at the wound on Ualan's leg. She needed to stop the bleeding, but if she touched him now…

Ualan's gurgled groans were muffled by the gag in his mouth. His eyes darted aimlessly around the room. His chest rose and fell and rapid, shallow breaths. Nanyehi needed to get as far away from here as possible. She needed to run. But she wasn't moving.

Ualan's hand swept through the air, and Nanyehi jumped back just in time to avoid making contact. In the dim moonlight she could see the tips of his fingers giving way to sharp, pointed claws. The transformation was starting. There was only one thing that could stop it now…

No, there were two things. Nanyehi looked at the knife still stuck in the wall. Ualan had sacrificed so much to save his brother from the curse, could Nanyehi really let it end like this?

Ualan shot up into a sitting position, blocking Nanyehi's

view of the knife. His hands gripped the back of his head. The gag strained against the tension of his elongating snout. He ripped it free with his razor sharp claws to reveal a mouth full of blood-drenched fangs cutting through his gums. Tufts of fur grew across his body. His bones contorted and twisted.

Never refuse help to a being in need. That's what Ualan said Ayita had taught him. That's what Nanyehi had been taught, as well. At least, so long as the being was one of her own.

Ualan turned his hungry, wolf-like eyes to Nanyehi as he rose to his feet. His form was almost unrecognizable. He leapt toward Nanyehi, his arms spread wide, his mouth agape. He was ready for the kill.

Fate had brought them together. Not just for the sake of Ualan's brother, but for Ualan himself.

Nanyehi dove forward, past Ualan's encroaching claws, and buried her face in his fur-covered chest, now torn free from his shirt. She wrapped her arms around him in a tight embrace.

Ualan's arms closed in on Nanyehi, and she gritted her teeth as his claws pierced through layers of leather and fabric to gently penetrate her skin. His hands scraped across her back, and the piercing, knife-like pain slowly gave way to the gentle pressure of Ualan's fingertips. The fur pressed against her face retreated into bare skin, and Ualan collapsed onto the floor, unconscious.

Nanyehi held her grip tight as his body writhed and twitched. Nanyehi clenched her eyes shut and listened only to the pounding in Ualan's chest until it slowed as he finally returned to his true form.

Nanyehi rose and examined him. His clothes were

ripped to shreds, and his leg was still bleeding. She tore a strip of Ualan's shirt and wrapped it around the wound. As she pulled it tight, Ualan jerked awake. His eyes filled with panic as they darted around the room.

"Be still." Nanyehi placed a hand on his chest. "You're going to be okay."

Ualan grabbed her arm. "You... you have to kill me!"

"I don't hate you that much." Nanyehi pulled Ualan up to a sitting position.

"No, I mean—" he gritted his teeth through the pain, "—I'm cursed." He scooted away from her and held up a hand to keep her back. "I don't want to hurt you! Please, before I turn..."

Did he really not remember anything that had just happened? That meant he didn't know...

Nanyehi stood and offered a hand to Ualan. "We have to get out of here before the others come," she said. "Can you walk?"

"What's the point?" Ualan looked up at her. The desperation in his voice was heartbreaking. "I don't... I don't have an angel."

So he didn't know the truth, after all. Nanyehi wanted to tell him, but the words stopped in her throat. She was still coming to grips with the choice she had made. Saying it out loud would make it real.

"We have a month to figure something out, don't we?" she lied. "Until then, you have to keep going for your brother." She pulled the silver knife from the wall, letting Lewis' body crumple to the floor. She held the blade up for Ualan to see. "We found exactly what we were looking for, didn't we?" She lifted Ualan to his feet and supported his weight as he reluctantly limped toward the door.

"I don't have an angel," he repeated.

In truth, the curse provided an angel for every werewolf, even those who were infected rather than moonborn. After they were bitten, a person was only without an angel until they physically touched a Human. It was how Sacagawea was bound to Lewis, even though she was so much younger than him.

In saving Ualan from Lewis' fatal claws, Nanyehi had become bound to him. As long as they were both alive, she would be his angel.

Chapter Six

Nanyehi was in a dark room. Every creak of the floorboards sent her spiraling in fear. Out of the shadows, a creature leaped, its claws extended...

THWACK!

Nanyehi awoke with a start as a sharp pain erupted from her cheek. She was on horseback, galloping at full speed through a dark wood. An unconscious Ualan lay in front of her, cradled in her arms as her hands reached around his limp body to grip the reins.

She must have dozed off while riding and slipped into a dream. But the pain felt so real...

She reached up and touched a finger to her cheek. Warm blood trickled down her hand. So, it hadn't been a dream.

She felt herself fighting exhaustion, struggling to recall the night's events. Had the werewolf attacked her, and she just hadn't remembered it? No, it was impossible. More likely, she had been startled awake by a stray branch overhanging the path.

She had managed to help Ualan limp down the hill, half-carrying him most of the way. As soon as they'd reached the lodge, she had thrown him onto the first horse she could find, jumped up behind him, and tore away from the inn as fast as the beast would carry them. She could remember desperately searching the tree line for any sign of an off-shooting path wide enough for a single horse to carry them away from the main road. Judging by how tightly the trees were encroaching on either side of her now, she gathered she must have found one.

She couldn't be sure how far behind any other guests from the inn were or if they were even following her. Surely they had heard the gunshot? She wondered if they had all been in on the secret, or if some had been destined to become unsuspecting victims of the werewolf's insatiable hunger. She thought back to the assortment of faces that sat around the small dining table. The only one that could have posed a threat was the satyr, and he was already dead. We're safe, Nanyehi assured herself.

She slowed the horse down and they continued at an even pace until they emerged into an open pasture illuminated by the first golden rays of dawn. The direction of the rising sun told her she'd been traveling roughly north-east. That was good to know. She made a mental note to check the map once she'd set up camp. Hopefully, she could get a general idea of where they'd landed. She slid down from the horse, careful to bring Ualan along without jostling him too much. She laid him down on a soft patch of moss. It was as comfortable as he could get, all things considered.

She took a moment to change the dressing on his wound, then stepped away from his subdued groans to take in the sounds of the peaceful landscape around them. In the distance, she could just make out the trickling cadence of running water. A stream! The thought of the cool, clear creek gently caressing her skin made her painfully aware of how uncomfortable she was in her stale, sweaty clothes. She grabbed the horse's reins and moved toward the source of the sound, but paused when she remembered Ualan. She couldn't leave him alone out in the open, could she?

Why not? It was the least he deserved after what he'd done to her. She took several more determined steps toward the forest edge before she stopped and growled. No, she couldn't just leave him. The fresh water would do him more good than it would her. Besides, it was unlikely he'd be waking up any time soon, so perhaps she could still take her bath with some semblance of privacy. She needed a moment alone to gather her thoughts.

She scooped Ualan up in her arms and marched into the woods. It didn't take long to find a small waterfall that emptied into a shallow basin surrounded by several rocky outcroppings. The horse nearly toppled over itself as it rushed to the edge of the pool for a drink. She found a perfect spot between two large rocks to deposit Ualan. This way most of his body would be submerged, without much risk of him slipping in too far. Plus, Nanyehi could position herself out of his line of sight should he happen to open his eyes.

She tore off the remains of his tattered shirt and tossed it aside. She would have to buy him a new one in the next town they visited. His denim jeans were still wearable, so she pulled them off and washed them in swirling, foamy water, then wrung them out and laid them on a sun-soaked rock to dry.

She moved around to the far side of the pool and repeated the process with her own garments. When she was finally, completely free, she slid down into the creek and let the gently flowing water lull her into a trance—keenly aware of its touch on every part of her body.

A small part of her almost wished Ualan would miraculously awaken and come wading across the pool. She chastised herself for even thinking it. Every *other* part of her wanted to hate him. He was directly—or perhaps only indirectly?—responsible for almost getting her killed. And yet, when the moment had come, she had chosen to save his life. She had decided to let him become a werewolf, knowing full well that meant she would be his angel. If they were stuck together for life anyway, why not consummate the relationship?

She opened her eyes. She could see most of his legs from this angle, but a well-placed boulder stopped her from seeing anything more. The knowledge that they were so close and exposed added fuel to the fire of that one small part's battle against her will to resist. Not that she could do anything about it at the moment. Ualan showed no signs of stirring.

Perhaps it was better this way. As young and naive as he was, he would likely make a clumsy and inexperienced lover. Even so, that one small part that longed for Ualan's touch was edging ever closer to victory. In the absence of Ualan's hand, she reached her own down to the spot and let her imaginary companion go to work.

~~ Chapter Seven ~~

Nanyehi removed the bandage from Ualan's leg. In the three days since the incident, she had worked diligently to keep the wound dressed and cleaned. Her efforts were paying off: there was no sign of infection, and the gash was already starting to heal. Nanyehi reached for the towel that waited beside a bowl of warm water on the bedside table.

When it had become clear no one from the inn was following them, Nanyehi had decided it would be best to care for Ualan in proper lodgings rather than drag him on horseback to a new, uniquely uncomfortable campsite night after night. It just so happened that the first city they came upon was Nashville.

Nanyehi was not accustomed to hiding in such a large city. She quickly learned there was a certain comfort in knowing you weren't the only stranger in town; not a single passer-by had given her or Ualan so much as a second glance. It might be the perfect opportunity for them to lay low even longer and give Ualan a chance to heal before they continued their travels. A wound like his could take years to recover from. In the meantime, they could blend right in with the locals; maybe Nanyehi could take on a job, and find them someplace more permanent to stay until...

No, Nanyehi chastised herself. She couldn't let herself think like that. It sounded too much like settling down. She grabbed the towel and soaked it in the warm water. She dabbed it on Ualan's wound, perhaps a bit more forcefully than she had intended.

"Ah!" Ualan called out. Nanyehi jerked, inflicting a fresh round of pain on Ualan's leg. He sat straight up in the bed. Over the past few days that Nanyehi had been caring for him, Ualan had only awakened a handful of times, each just long enough for her to force some cold soup down his throat before he slipped back into unconsciousness. She grabbed a cup of broth she had ready for just such an opportunity.

"Drink this," she held it up to his lips, "you need your strength."

He took several heavy gulps of the liquid, then lowered the glass to his lap. Nanyehi watched in anticipation as—rather than collapse back onto his pillow—he stared around the room through hazy eyes.

"What... where..." he shook his head and blinked. "What happened?"

"We..." Nanyehi paused, unsure of how detailed an explanation to give. He'd asked the same question a half-dozen times—it was unlikely he would remember any of it the next time he woke up. "You were attacked," she answered.

"Attacked?" Ualan squinted into a distant corner of

the room. Nanyehi returned to her work, and Ualan's gaze made its lumbering way to the spot on his leg.

"By a werewolf," Nanyehi stated, not looking up from her work.

Ualan grabbed Nanyehi's wrist, and her eyes shot up to meet his. His gaze held perfect clarity and understanding. She realized that Ualan was not falling back asleep this time.

"You didn't… you let…" Ualan struggled to find the words.

"It was the Satyr," Nanyehi said. "He grabbed you from the cabin and threw you in with—"

"You should have let me die," Ualan said. Nanyehi searched his eyes. He was genuinely terrified.

"We made a deal," Nanyehi said. "You think I was gonna let you out of it that easily?" Of course, there was more to it than that, but Nanyehi wasn't ready to admit that to herself, much less to Ualan. "Besides," Nanyehi continued, "your brother still needs you. Isn't that reason enough to keep living?"

Ualan sighed and collapsed back onto the bed. Nanyehi set back to work redressing his wound. "So Halfy is a werewolf?" Ualan asked.

"*Was* a werewolf," Nanyehi clarified. "And 'Halfy' was Meriwether Lewis."

"No way," Ualan looked up. "He was still alive after all this time?"

"And he took out a few werewolf hunters over the years, too." She grabbed the knife from her belt. "That's how I found this. He kept a trophy collection."

"Silver that killed a werewolf," Ualan said as the realization dawned on him.

"Silver that killed a werewolf," Nanyehi confirmed. She finished wrapping Ualan's wound and lowered his pant leg to cover the bandage. "We can perform the ritual whenever you're ready."

Ualan sat up in his bed. "We find my brother his angel, and then I want you to use that knife on me."

"No!" Nanyehi reflexively moved the blade out of Ualan's sight. "I'm not going to—"

"I don't have an angel, Nanyehi," Ualan insisted. "I wasn't born with the curse—"

"There's more to the curse than you know," Nanyehi cut him off.

"And what's that?"

"I… I can't tell you," Nanyehi turned away. "Not yet."

"Please," Ualan pressed. "Nanyehi."

Her name on his lips twisted her stomach. She looked away. "I need you to focus on helping your brother," she lied. "We can find—" she paused, "—your angel. Later." She knew full well that she was his angel, but if he knew that too, it would only distract him from the mission. At least, that's what she kept telling herself. She got up from her chair and rummaged through her satchel.

"I have an angel?" Ualan shook his head. "But I wasn't born like this."

"Just know that you're safe for now." Nanyehi pulled the ingredients free. "I know I'm asking a lot, but I need you to trust me."

Ualan studied her in silence for a long time, then nodded. "So, how does the ritual work?"

Nanyehi revealed the objects she had been searching for: a map and a pipe. "First, we smoke," she said as she set the pipe on the edge of Ualan's bed and spread the map at his feet. "A mixture of your brother's hair and some, shall we say, very 'potent' herbs. Then we both take hold of the knife while we wait for the visions to start. We'll see where the knife dropped when we wake up, and that will be our destination."

"When we wake up?" Ualan asked.

"Like I said," Nanyehi answered, "Very potent herbs." She removed a small pouch from her belt and stuffed the matted, green contents into the chamber of her pipe. She held out a hand to Ualan. He looked at her open hand, then back up at her. "The hair," Nanyehi prompted.

"Right." Ualan searched around, then spotted his belongings on a table by his bedside. He grabbed the small pouch and handed Nanyehi a tangled mess of bloody hair.

"You could have cleaned it," Nanyehi scowled.

"I didn't want to take any chances," Ualan replied. "What if you needed the blood?"

Nanyehi stuffed it into the pipe, then struck a match. "This is about to be the worst thing you've smelled in your life," she said.

"I grew up on a farm—" The smoke hit his nostrils, and he turned away with something between a cough and a wretch.

"I warned you," Nanyehi said. She took a long drag from the pipe, held it in her mouth, then tilted her head back and blew the smoke toward the ceiling. She passed the pipe to Ualan, who took it with a skeptical scowl. "For your brother," Nanyehi prompted.

"For my brother," Ualan said. His lips had barely touched the lip of the pipe before he started hacking and sputtering.

"Don't worry," Nanyehi comforted him. "You get used

to it after the first three or four pulls."

"Three or four?" Ualan coughed out between shallow breaths. "How long are we smoking this thing?"

"Till it's gone," Nanyehi shrugged. "Or you start seeing things that aren't there, whichever comes first."

Ualan waved a hand through the black haze that had formed between them. "Can't see a thing through this rancid smoke," he said.

"Then when you start seeing again, you'll know the ritual's working," Nanyehi said.

Ualan made another attempt at the pipe and held it down for several seconds before practically throwing it back at Nanyehi. She took it, inhaled deeply, and relished making Ualan squirm as she blew the smoke much closer to his face this time.

"Now you're just torturing me," he spat.

"I'd be lying if I said I wasn't enjoying myself," she admitted. She passed the pipe back to Ualan, and he took a decently long, full drag. "You know," Nanyehi said as she took the pipe back from Ualan, "if you do join me as an angel hunter—"

"I've got a lot more of this to look forward to, don't I?" he asked.

"A lot more," Nanyehi smirked.

"Still no visions," Ualan announced.

"Don't worry," Nanyehi chided, "it won't be much longer now."

Neither spoke as they continued passing the pipe for several more rounds. When the room's silence grew as thick as the fog, Nanyehi said, "Tell me more about your brother."

"He's a good kid," Ualan shrugged. "Barely twelve

years old, and he's already got more of a head for running the farm than I ever did."

"Then it's a good thing he's the one who stayed home, eh?" Nanyehi teased.

"Yeah, I suppose it is. Not that I'm much good at this, either."

"You know," Nanyehi diverted, "you never told me his name."

Ualan chuckled and shook his head. "It's kind of embarrassing."

"Embarrassing? How so?"

"Well, my father never gave him a name before he left, and my mom, well, you know—"

"Wait," Nanyehi held up a hand. "Did you name your brother?"

"Uh, I kind of did by accident, yeah."

Nanyehi shook her head incredulously. "How do you name a kid by accident?"

"Well, everyone around me kept saying things like, 'The boy is moonborn.'"

Nanyehi gasped. "You didn't."

"Well, when they said he needed a name, I just thought—"

"You did. You named your brother Moonborn, didn't you?"

Ualan pursed his lips and raised his hands in surrender. "Yeah. I named my brother Moonborn."

Nanyehi burst into laughter. Perhaps a bit more intensely than she would have under normal circumstances, but that was one side-effect of the ritual.

Ualan's eyes glazed over and fixed on something in the distance. Before Nanyehi could comment, he asked, "What does it mean when I see someone walking behind you?"

Nanyehi glanced over her shoulder. There was no one there. "That depends, who do you see?"

"I don't know…some kind of Fae. Or maybe an Elf?

"What do they look like?"

"Pointy ears, really tall, black and white robes, condescending glare…"

"Definitely an Elf. I think it's time to grab the knife," she answered. She took hold of the handle and held it with the blade facing down toward the map. Ualan wrapped his hand around hers.

"So, we just hold it here, like this?" he asked.

Nanyehi hesitated. She wasn't sure if it was the warmth of his touch or the herbs that made her heart beat faster. "What do you see?" she asked when she snapped back to reality.

"Elves, all women," Ualan answered. "Nuns, maybe?"

Nanyehi's stomach dropped. She knew exactly where this was heading. "What else do you see?" she asked.

"I see…" His eyes were darting all around the room. "I see…"

As his voice faded, Nanyehi's visions set in. A large brick building with ominous turrets. Elves in austere black-and-white garments. Human children gathered around a crucifix with the image of a bloody, beaten Faun. A young girl, her dark braid being harshly undone by one elf as a second struck the girl's hands with a ruler.

"That's her," Nanyehi said. "Remember her face."

"I see…" Ualan's voice sounded miles away.

Nanyehi grew dizzy as she flew through the school halls and then out onto the grounds. Deep in the woods, she rushed past a Gargoyle pushing a wheelbarrow. The last thing she saw before blacking out was a field covered in mounds of freshly turned dirt.

Nanyehi awoke with a start. Dim light from the waning gibbous moon shone through the window. It was the middle of the night.

Nanyehi checked the map. The knife lay on its side, a clear hole marking the spot where she and Ualan had dropped it. Their destination was in Canada. The journey would take three weeks at least, with only one horse between them. They would be arriving just in time for the next full moon. Nanyehi considered waking Ualan to get started right away; the sooner they headed out, the better. As she placed a hand on his shoulder to shake him, she reconsidered. He did need all the rest he could get. Perhaps waiting until morning would be the better option, after all.

Nanyehi pulled the covers up over Ualan, then carefully folded the map and packed up her things. She sat down on the cot she had made for herself on the floor. It was a frigid evening, and the pull of the soft bed was more than a little tempting. Especially considering the bed also contained a warm body to help chase away the chill.

Nanyehi shivered, then slid under the covers of her cot. There was no point in spoiling herself with a comfortable bed the night before going out on the trail. The journey would be rough, but if she was tough enough to handle it, she was certainly tough enough to handle one more night on the hard floor.

"So, the vision," Ualan said as he settled down on the opposite side of the campfire to Nanyehi. "It seems like we're heading to some sort of school?"

It was nearly a week into their journey, and Nanyehi had barely spoken more than was necessary to keep them moving forward on the right path. She certainly didn't want to talk about what they were about to face. "A residential school, yes."

Ualan was silent for several moments, and Nanyehi hoped that was the end of it. When he finally spoke again, it was with a soft, genuinely curious voice. "The nuns… why were they pulling down the girl's hair?"

Nanyehi spat. "To erase her identity. To make her forget her own culture."

In the flicker of firelight, Nanyehi could see Ualan's eyes begin to water. He swallowed hard as if choking back emotion. "Those kids were taken from their families, weren't they?"

Nanyehi shook her head. "Worse, their parents were likely murdered by the same creatures that now claim to be their saviors. They only care about the children. It's much easier to indoctrinate innocent minds."

Ualan leaned forward and rested his face in his hands. "I've never understood what some people are willing to do in the name of their religion."

"It isn't even *their* religion!" Nanyehi nearly shot up out of her seat. "I mean, it would be bad enough if they were trying to teach us about their Elvish gods, but no!

They worship some desert Faun who got himself killed two thousand years ago and probably never even set foot in Europe!"

Ualan seemed taken aback by her outburst but still looked on with eyes that sympathized with her pain. "Have you found angels in schools like this often?"

Nanyehi took a deep breath to rein herself in. "No, this is the first time."

Ualan's brow furrowed. "I'm surprised to hear that."

"Up till now, I've always found them living with their family in some remote tribe, or on a reservation the benevolent government was generous enough to gift us."

Ualan chuckled at her sarcastic remark. "Ironic, considering they stole the land from you in the first place."

Nanyehi rolled her eyes. "The werewolf and their family will typically relocate and join the angel's tribe."

"And the new tribe accepts them, just like that?"

"It hasn't always been this way," Nanyehi explained. "In the days of my ancestors, a werewolf and their angel would often come from separate, warring nations. The angel hunter would take a child against their will, the angel's tribe would retaliate, and so the conflict would continue to escalate."

"Huh," Ualan cocked his head. "I thought the whole point of the curse was to put an end to all the fighting. To stop the nations from stealing each other's lands."

"Well, maybe a curse that forced sworn enemies to kidnap each other's children wasn't the best way to go about that."

"So why are the different nations so willing to help each other now? What changed?"

"We all have a common enemy now, that's what

changed."

"Ah, right. People like me."

"No, not like—" Nanyehi bit her tongue. She was surprised to realize she had become so comfortable talking to Ualan, that she had almost forgotten she was sitting across from a colonizer. He had once said he felt more Human than Fae. It seemed that whether she liked it or not, Nanyehi was beginning to think of him that way, as well. "The point is, this job is different from anything I've done before. Now if you don't mind, I'm going to get some rest. We have a long day ahead of us tomorrow."

As she made her way toward her cot, she heard Ualan mutter, "I'm afraid we have a lot of long days ahead of us."

Chapter Eight

Even after three weeks, the image had remained seared in Nanyehi's mind; an ever-present beacon prodding her to strive on, day and night, until she reached her destination. The stoic brick building loomed tall and imposing as it had been in the vision. Ualan was determined to save his brother; Nanyehi was determined to rescue the girl from this cesspit. She would take all the children out from under these colonizers' oppression if she could, but she knew that was wishful thinking at best.

"Lost, are you?" a voice as hard as stone called out from somewhere on the grounds. Nanyehi spotted a grotesque, winged creature stepping out from a flower garden, shovel in hand. He pierced his shovel into the ground and hobbled toward them.

"Is that… a demon?" Ualan asked. "What sort of place is this?"

"A gargoyle," Nanyehi corrected him. "They often

watch over churches and schools like this. They can sit still as statues for hours on end, and nothing gets past them."

Ualan scoffed. "It appears this guard dog is doubling as the groundskeeper."

"So it would seem," Nanyehi muttered under her breath as the gargoyle approached.

"This is a private institution," the gargoyle barked. "We don't allow visitors."

"I'm here to see my niece," Nanyehi lied. "Her name is…" Nanyehi paused. In all her years of playing cards, she had never played a bluff as big as this one. If her hunch was correct, the odds were in her favor. "…Ayita," she finished. She caught a very brief, very puzzled look from Ualan in the corner of her eye. She almost imperceptibly turned the palm of her hand in his direction to subtly reassure him. *Trust me*, she thought in his direction. *I know what I'm doing. I hope.*

The gargoyle spat on the ground. "You think that means anything to me?" he asked. "We don't use their Vanaran names here."

Nanyehi gritted her teeth. Her hunch had been right, after all.

"The Headmistress'll want to hear about this," the gargoyle continued as he turned and headed back up the path toward the school. "Can't make any promises she'll let you see the girl, though."

Nanyehi and Ualan followed him up the path in strained silence. As they drew near the building, Nanyehi looked into the garden and spotted an ornate bench nestled among an alcove of rose bushes. On the bench sat a young girl of about twelve, who was reading from a leather-bound book with a flowing, silk bookmark.

"That's her," Ualan whispered. Her hair was cut to shoulder length, and the peaceful tranquility on her face was a far cry from the pained expression she had borne in the vision, but there was no mistaking it: She was Moonborn's angel.

"We'll just wait out here," Nanyehi called ahead to the gargoyle as he mounted the slate stone steps of the school's entrance. "We wouldn't want to cause a… commotion."

The gargoyle turned back with a leery side-eye. "Probably for the best," he muttered before he pushed open the heavy oak doors and disappeared inside.

Nanyehi and Ualan slipped into the garden as soon as they were alone. "Hello," Nanyehi said as they approached the girl.

"Hmm?" the girl jumped and slammed her book closed.

"I'm sorry," Nanyehi retreated, "I didn't mean to startle you."

"It's alrigth," the girl's timid voice replied. "It's just I…" Her eyes darted back and forth between them. "We're not used to visitors here."

"I understand." Nanyehi crouched down to the girl's level. "Can you tell me your name?"

The girl looked down and twirled the silk bookmark between her fingers. "Christine," she said.

Nanyehi placed a gentle hand on the girl's knee. "No, I mean your real name."

The girl's brow furrowed. "My real name?" she asked.

"You know," Nanyehi prodded, "the one your parents—" At the mere mention of the word, the girl's eyes grew wide.

"Her parents," a matronly voice with a thick, French

accent called out from behind them, "were killed when she was little more than a babe." Nanyehi shot up and spun around to see a stern, regal elf gliding down the garden path. She was easily a foot taller than Nanyehi.

The gargoyle shuffled alongside her, struggling to match her leisurely pace with his short legs. "These, Headmistress Augustine, are the visitors I was telling you about."

"Thank you, Constant." The Headmistress waved a hand, ushering the diminutive creature to slink out of sight. She turned her attention back to Nanyehi. "Another Vanaran tribe attacked her village. We rescued as many of the children as we could. I shudder to think what the savages would have done…" she stopped short with a compassionate look in Christine's direction. "It is by God's grace alone that she is with us now."

"And now she can be with me," Nanyehi said. "We can be a family again."

Headmistress Augustine cocked her head. "Are you saying you want to take the child with you?"

Before Nanyehi could answer, Ualan stepped forward. "I know this must all seem very unusual," he said. Nanyehi wanted to shove him out of the way, but her better judgment told her that having someone of European descent speak on her behalf was the better option. "It's just that this girl—Christine—is the only family my companion has left."

"Yes," the Headmistress mused. "My groundskeeper, Constant, told me you claimed the girl was your niece."

Christine looked up at Nanyehi. "I never knew I had—"

"I've been away for many years traveling," Nanyehi

interjected. "But I'm back now, and I want—"

The Headmistress turned to Ualan. "And you," she said, "do you vouch for this woman?"

"She has served as a guide on many of my expeditions. I consider her as trustworthy as my own kin."

Nanyehi couldn't suppress a slight smirk. As far as lies went, that one wasn't half bad.

Christine rose from her bench and stood dutifully at the Headmistress' side. "May I say something, Headmistress?" she asked.

"Of course, child," the Headmistress answered.

"It's just, well…" Christine looked up at Nanyehi with an almost guilty expression. "It's just that I don't want to leave."

Nanyehi's eyes widened in shock. How could she not want to leave? Didn't she understand what the Elves were doing to her? To her people?

"I completely understand, dear," the Headmistress said with a tone of finality. "No one can force you to leave if you don't want to."

"But she has to," Nanyehi's head was reeling. "I'm her… she's…" Of all the obstacles Nanyehi had prepared for, the girl's unwillingness to cooperate had not been one of them.

"Perhaps a compromise?" The Headmistress raised a hand, stopping Nanyehi's advance. She hadn't even realized she'd been edging ever closer to the child.

"A compromise?" Nanyehi turned the word over as if trying to understand how it fit in this context.

"We will allow you to remain on the premises for one day," the Headmistress continued, ignoring Nanyehi's confusion. "You will see that the children here are well taken care of and provided for. Perhaps you will see that Christine should remain here rather than be turned over to your dubitable care. Should Christine change her mind, she may accompany you. Either way, by this time tomorrow, you will leave us in peace."

Nanyehi didn't think it sounded so much like a compromise as a list of demands, and a rather condescending one at that. "I can't just stand by and—"

Ualan placed a hand on Nanyehi's shoulder. "We accept your compromise," he said. Nanyehi shot him an ice-cold glare, and he matched it with a determined look of his own. "One day," he insisted.

Nanyehi took a deep breath. Right, of course, she hadn't been thinking straight. This gave them twenty-four hours to come up with a plan. They had to think of something, anything. Twenty-four hours was better than nothing. "Okay," Nanyehi conceded. "We'll stay."

"Very well," the Headmistress seemed to straighten up even taller than before. Nanyehi couldn't help but think she was gloating at her victory. "I will be sure to have your rooms prepared as soon as possible. Lunch will be served at the bell—"

"We wouldn't mind sharing a room," Nanyehi shot a deceitfully innocent look in Ualan's direction. "If it's easier for you."

"Oh?" The Headmistress looked Ualan up and down as if reassessing her opinion of him. "I was not aware the two of you were married."

"Well, we—" Ualan started, but Nanyehi jumped in before he could finish.

"We're not," she blurted out. "It's just that we don't want to be an inconvenience, that's all. We've grown quite accustomed to sharing quarters on our travels."

Nanyehi could almost hear Ualan gritting his teeth. One glance at the Headmistress confirmed she had just made a terrible mistake.

"I'm not sure what the customs of…" the Headmistress raised her eyebrows, "…your people are, but in a house of the Lord the unwed shall remain separated."

Before Nanyehi could open her mouth to speak, the Headmistress turned and marched back to the school, Christine matching her pace perfectly.

A few hours later, Nanyehi and Ualan were roaming the quiet, austere halls alone. The children were all eating lunch. Nanyehi and Ualan had elected to eat from their rations in their rooms rather than join the others in the cafeteria. This gave them some extra time to snoop around.

"There's one more issue we need to address," Ualan was saying.

"Hmm?" Nanyehi was only half listening. There was an open door just ahead, and she thought she heard mumbling from that direction.

"Tonight is the full moon," Ualan said.

Nanyehi looked down at the floor and suppressed a curse. She had been delaying the conversation as long as possible. Perhaps too long. "There's more to the curse than I've told you about," Nanyehi started.

Before she could muster the courage to tell him the

truth, Ualan cut in, "You still have the silver knife." He had already decided how this conversation would go and wouldn't hear anything Nanyehi had to say. "You can't let me transform, not here. Not with all these—"

"It won't come to that," Nanyehi assured him. "I told you. I need you to trust—" She stopped short the moment she caught a glimpse inside the open door. An Elf holding a steaming bowl of soup stood over a bed. On the bed lay a frail Human boy who looked like he hadn't eaten in days. On the other side of the bed stood the Headmistress, dangling a crucifix on a chain inches from the boy's face.

"I want to let you eat. I do. You're only doing this to yourself—"

The Headmistress' dull monotone was interrupted by a sharp intake of breath from the second Elf, who had spotted Nanyehi and Ualan in the hall. "Headmistress!" she hissed in a whisper.

The Headmistress turned and spotted the pair of visitors outside the room. She swiftly stepped to the door and pushed it closed, leaving Nanyehi and Ualan alone in the oppressive silence of the hall.

Nanyehi felt if she stood there a moment longer, she might vomit. "Let's go outside. I need some fresh air."

Chapter Nine

"I thought we might find you here," Nanyehi said as they approached Christine, sitting on the same garden bench and reading the same book as before.

"Oh, hi." She looked down at the ground and closed her book—slowly this time. "I've finished my classes for the day, so I wanted to practice my verses before dinner."

"Your verses?" Ualan asked.

Christine looked up and, without opening her book, recited, "If my people, which are called by my name, shall humble themselves, and pray, and seek my face, and turn from their wicked ways; then will I hear from heaven, and will forgive—"

Nanyehi couldn't stand to listen a second longer. "And what happens when you don't pray?"

Christine gasped, and her gaze retreated to the security of the book in her lap. "Sometimes…" she seemed on the edge of some dire confession but afraid of what punishment she might receive.

"They don't let you eat?" Nanyehi prompted.

"Nanyehi—" Ualan placed a hand on her shoulder.

Nanyehi shrugged him off. She needed to know the truth, all of it. More importantly, she needed Christine to say it out loud. To understand how important it was that she leave this place.

As if in response to Nanyehi's advance, Christine's defenses went up. "I do love it here," she insisted. "They treat us all very well. It's only the naughty kids..." Her knuckles turned white as her grip tightened around the binding of her Bible.

Nanyehi knelt in front of Christine and placed a gentle hand on hers, and her fingers seemed to relax. Nanyehi knew she was on the edge of a breakthrough. "What happens to the naughty kids?"

"They just... disappear."

"Such vivid imaginations these children have," the Headmistress' cold voice cut through their quiet moment.

Nanyehi jumped to her feet.

"Such fanciful stories they tell."

Nanyehi gritted her teeth. "Seems like more than just a story to me."

The Headmistress gave a dismissive wave. "All a misunderstanding, I'm sure."

Christine stood and looked at the Headmistress with conflicted eyes as if wanting to believe but needing confirmation. "There was a boy in my class, Jean Baptiste."

"There are many boys named Jean Baptiste at this school," the Headmistress answered. "It is a strong, Christian name."

"He was in *my* class!" Christine persisted.

"Perhaps he was moved to a different class. It happens quite often. Now come, Christine, it's time we went inside."

"Yes, Headmistress," Christine said as she lowered her head and obediently followed.

Once again, Nanyehi and Ualan were left standing alone, empty-handed.

"Let's take a walk," Ualan said. Once they had rounded a corner of climbing rose bushes, Ualan spoke again. "It has to be tonight."

"What?" Nanyehi had been lost in thought, making plans of her own. She still hadn't found a way to tell him.

"Next chance we get, we should grab the girl and run," Ualan continued. "We only have a few hours left before… before the moon rises."

It's now or never. "I told you, you don't have to worry about that."

"You haven't told me anything," Ualan countered. "As far as I'm concerned, we need to be as far away from this place as possible before I—"

"You aren't going to transform," Nanyehi said.

"How? I don't have an angel."

"I'm your angel!" she snapped.

Ualan stopped dead in his tracks and turned to look at Nanyehi, eyes wide and mouth agape. "What?"

The confession had escaped Nanyehi's lips far easier than she had anticipated. She turned and placed her hands on Ualan's shoulders. "When a person receives the curse from a werewolf bite, the next human who touches them becomes their angel. I am your angel." She emphasized the last words to assure herself of their truth as much as Ualan.

"Hm," Ualan diverted his gaze thoughtfully. "So that's

why you wanted to share a room."

"Yeah, I messed that one up pretty bad, didn't it?" Nanyehi cringed.

"You didn't know," Ualan said. "Besides, we still have a few hours to sneak you into my room."

His sly smirk elicited a chuckle from Nanyehi. "I'm sure we won't be the only ones sneaking around tonight."

"Though for slightly different reasons, of course."

Nanyehi quickly removed her hands from Ualan's shoulders. "Oh, of course."

Ualan cocked his head and raised his eyebrows. "Because for a minute there, I thought you wanted to share a room so we could finish what we started at—"

"Of course not." Nanyehi shook her head and continued walking along the garden path. "Hadn't even crossed my mind." In truth, it hadn't. She'd been so preoccupied with finding a way to get Christine away from the school she hadn't even considered what else the night may bring. Now that she *was* thinking about it, it sounded like a welcome distraction.

"Well, if you're that eager—" Ualan gestured to the tall shrubbery around them, "—we've got plenty of privacy out—"

Nanyehi rounded another corner, then froze. In the distance, the gargoyle had his back to her and was dropping a large, cloth-covered figure into a wheelbarrow. She hissed a sharp intake of breath, then ducked back behind the corner. She grabbed Ualan's arm and pulled him out of sight with her.

"Whoa," Ualan caught his balance just before his back slammed into a thorny bush. "I wasn't being serious—"

Nanyehi clasped a hand over his mouth. "Not that!

Look!"

Ualan followed her nod around the corner, watched for a moment, and then came back around.

Nanyehi's eyes were locked on him as his fingers massaged the corners of his jaw. "We both know where that wheelbarrow is headed and exactly what... *who* is in it."

"The field from the vision," Ualan muttered.

"So you saw it, too."

"I didn't want to believe it."

"It has to be tonight," Nanyehi said.

"What?"

"We grab the girl, and we run." Nanyehi turned to march back to the school.

Ualan grabbed her arm and pulled her back. "We can't. There's no way we can get far enough away before the moon rises."

"Then we keep going."

"How?" Ualan turned his wrist out toward her. "Tied together, wrangling a girl who doesn't want to leave home?"

"She'll want to leave after we show her—"

"We can't show her."

Nanyehi's eyes darted back and forth between Ualan's. She was too stunned to speak.

"She can never know."

"Like hell she can't!" Nanyehi cried.

Ualan cringed and looked around. "Keep your voice down!"

"If she doesn't know, she'll spend her whole life thinking we kidnapped her from some kind of paradise. She'll hate us for—"

"And if she does know," Ualan cut her off, "she'll spend her whole life knowing she left her friends to die."

Nanyehi clenched her jaw. The weight of the decision came crashing down on her. Either option would have terrible ramifications for Christine, and she alone would bear the consequences of Nanyehi's choice for as long as she lived. One way or the other, Christine had to leave this place; for her own sake as much as for Ualan's brother.

"Now's our chance," Ualan's gentle voice intruded on her thoughts. "While that little imp is busy. We'll go inside and tell them we'll have dinner in our rooms. Other than that, we stay out of the way and don't say a word. Once you've had time to clear your thoughts, find a way to slip out and—"

Nanyehi shook her head. "I'm in no state to—"

Ualan shushed her with a finger on her lips. "If either of us can make this work, we both know it has to be you."

Chapter Ten

Ualan had been right, and Nanyehi had known it. She'd returned to her room in too much of a haze to do or say anything rash—though she'd certainly imagined plenty of things she *could* have said or done. She'd forced down as much food as her twisted stomach would allow, then slipped quietly out the window. Getting *out* of her room was a simpler task than Nanyehi had anticipated. Either the Elves were too trusting of the students, or the Gargoyle provided enough deterrent to keep the kids from even trying it. In that case, Nanyehi knew she needed to get around to Ualan's room before the watchdog finished his business in the woods.

Moving through the gardens that sprawled around the entire compound proved a far more straightforward task than sneaking through dense forest. The hedges were tall enough to obscure her from the view of any windows, though an eagle-eyed sentry perched on the roof would have spotted her easily enough. She moved quickly and quietly along the well-beaten path and paused at corners just long enough to ensure she wouldn't be emerging into any surprise encounters.

She kept a wary eye on the distant tree line as often as she could, watching for any sign of the Gargoyle returning from his grim duty. At last, she spotted Ualan's marked window. She slipped her fingers between the cracked panes and pulled them open.

Ualan was waiting inside and quickly pulled her in. He latched the window behind her and closed the curtains, never releasing his grip on her arm.

Nanyehi looked down with a smug grin at the hand that clenched her wrist. "The moon's not out yet."

"I know. I'm sorry," Ualan said, still not breaking contact. "I've just been sitting here thinking it would be any minute now. Every tingle down my leg or itch between my shoulders has me convinced it's starting."

Nanyehi pulled her arm free. "We still have an hour, at least."

Ualan's fingers flexed open and closed, searching for something to hold. "It's just… you know. My first time being a werewolf."

Nanyehi raised her eyebrows and shrugged. "And it's my first time being an angel." She sat in a chair by a writing desk.

Ualan sat on the edge of the bed. "Moonborn will be getting locked up right about now."

"It's the last time he'll have to go through that," Nanyehi said.

Ualan shook his head. "We're so close. If we had just made it here a few days earlier…"

"It's the last time," Nanyehi insisted. "That's what matters."

"You haven't seen it… the fear in his eyes—"

"I've seen it more times than I can count," Nanyehi retorted. "I've been in the room when someone chained to a chair transforms so I can take a clump of their fur. It's the same fear in all of their eyes. Fear of what they might do, of who they might hurt. Fear of what they are becoming."

Ualan's gaze fell to the floor. "He's my kid brother."

Nanyehi stood from her chair and marched across the room. She placed a hand on Ualan's cheek and guided his eyes up to meet hers. "Do you know what else I've seen? I've seen them put it in the past. I've seen the relief in their eyes the first time they look up at a full moon and realize they will *never* become that beast again. That's what we're giving to Moonborn. We're giving him the rest of his life. Everything else will be just a memory."

Nanyehi wasn't sure if she pulled Ualan's face toward hers or if he rose of his own volition. All she knew was that their lips were touching, and she had no intention of pushing him away. Her hand on his cheek slid to the back of his head; loose hair caressing the gaps between her fingers.

Her free hand found the small of his back and pulled his waist tight against hers. Ualan's hands did the same, and the pressure of their bodies against each other was immensely satisfying. At the same time, it made her hungry to be even closer.

Both of her hands moved toward Ualan's front and met at the top button of his shirt. Her fingers longed to brush the smooth skin of his chest and trace the muscles running down his stomach. Nanyehi finished the last button and threw the two panels of fabric apart.

Ualan's arms moved back to let his shirt fall free, then quickly returned and set to work on Nanyehi's top. Before her undergarments had time to hit the floor, he spun her around and threw her bare back against the bed. Their lips were barely parted for a moment before Ualan climbed on top of her and resumed their passionate interplay. Each deep breath pressed their bodies closer together—bare skin against bare skin.

Ualan's kiss traveled to Nanyehi's cheek, then to her ear. She turned her head to give his lips an open path down her neck and onto her chest. His hands massaged the bottoms of her breasts, and the relief they brought was as relaxing as it was arousing.

Nanyehi felt herself becoming completely disarmed under the influence of Ualan's touch. Either he wasn't the naive, inexperienced lover Nanyehi had assumed, or he was acting on pure animal instinct—and his instincts were delivering exactly what Nanyehi wanted.

Nanyehi moaned as Ualan's lips clenched tightly around one nipple, and his fingers simultaneously pinched the other. As his hand twisted and prodded on the first side, his tongue copied its movements on the second.

The more Nanyehi writhed in pleasure, the more her heavy jeans grew unbearably uncomfortable. She forced her hands underneath Ualan to undo her belt, then pushed his shoulders down, prompting him to finish the job. She lifted her hips as his fingers slipped beneath her waistband. She had only a moment to bask in the freedom of open air before Ualan's tongue returned to work. As her senses soared, she clenched her eyes shut to keep from being completely overwhelmed. Her fingers gripped the bed sheets, and her leg wrapped around Ualan's back, forcing him even closer in.

Just when Nanyehi felt she couldn't handle more, Ualan pushed himself away. The sound of his pants hitting the floor prompted Nanyehi to open her eyes, and her vision was flooded with a swirl of luminescent color. As he crawled back onto the bed, Nanyehi saw two shimmering beams protruding from just beneath his shoulder blades, pulsating back and forth. She reached out a hand to touch them, but they passed right through—like wings made of pure light.

She was so enamored with the illusion she barely noticed Ualan slide between her legs—or the bed fall away beneath them. The entire world could have collapsed beneath their feet, and she wouldn't have known the difference.

They were floating.

Ualan's hips started moving and sent them careening around the room in a tangled flight of passion and sweat. Nanyehi secretly wished they would slam full force into a wall, but Ualan maintained enough control to pull them up short each time they came close.

They found their way over the bed, and Nanyehi took advantage of her chance to throw Ualan's back against the mattress. Once again connected to a stable surface, Nanyehi gained the leverage to thrust her hips in time with Ualan's.

With one of his hands clenching her waist and the other squeezing her breast, Ualan moaned.

It was the sound of her name on his strained voice that sent her over the edge. Waves of pleasure washed through her like fire in her veins as she howled in ecstasy and collapsed onto Ualan's chest.

His hands continued to guide her hips back and forth as he thrust into her harder than ever, building to his climax. When he finished, they both deflated, and his lips softly brushed against her cheek. It was as gentle a kiss as she had ever received; as small and simple and sincere as the first drop of rain falling on a drought-parched land.

She melted into his arms, and they both lay perfectly still, basking in the afterglow of their luminous passion. Nanyehi knew they would eventually have to bind themselves together for the night or risk losing contact while they slept, allowing Ualan to transform. For the time being, however, there was no chance that a single inch of Nanyehi's skin would be separated from Ualan's.

When she finally found her voice again, Nanyehi said, "We still have so much to do. We have to find a way to get Christine out of here."

"About that," Ualan replied. "I think I have a plan."

Chapter Eleven

"After breakfast, I'd like to show you something," Nanyehi said to Christine, who sat across from her with her head down, quietly eating her oatmeal.

"I look forward to it," she replied in a voice that implied she didn't.

Nanyehi couldn't be sure if she was feigning interest to appease the intruding stranger or if she was simply too intimidated by the Headmistress to let her true excitement show.

"In the woods on the way in," Nanyehi explained, "I saw some herbs our people use for their medicinal qualities. I'd like to teach you our family's special way of preparing them—"

As expected, the Headmistress' cold voice cut over Nanyehi's shoulder. "Your primitive rituals will not be practiced on these sacred grounds."

Nanyehi looked to Ualan for support. She knew better

than to argue the point herself this time around.

He picked up his cue without hesitation. "Oh, it's not magic at all. I've used the herbs myself many times on our expeditions. It's truly amazing how God's creations can be used in such miraculous ways."

The Headmistress squinted. She had not been expecting such a well-reasoned counter. "Even so, I don't think—"

"Perhaps," Christine interjected in a small, timid voice, barely loud enough for the Headmistress to hear, "it would be an educational experience. That is, to study it from a scientific perspective."

Nanyehi turned her head away from the Headmistress to hide her smirk. So, the girl was curious about her family history after all. That was precisely the hook she needed.

"Very well," Headmistress Augustine conceded. "I shall send Constant with you as a chaperone."

"That's perfect," Nanyehi agreed, much to the Headmistress' surprise. "Perhaps he can bring back a sample to cultivate in your gardens." She and Ualan had predicted they would never be allowed to take Christine into the woods alone. Better to make ditching the gargoyle part of the plan than to risk not being able to get the girl away from the school at all. "We'll leave right after breakfast. When we're done, Constant can escort Christine back to the school, and we'll be on our way."

Headmistress Augustine nodded. "I wish you well on your travels."

"Which way to these herbs?" Constant stepped out past the outermost edge of the gardens while Nanyehi, Ualan, and Christine stopped short behind him.

Nanyehi looked to the east, toward where she had seen the gargoyle haul his wheelbarrow just the night before. Ualan gave her a warning glance. There were more than enough reasons not to send the party in that direction. For one, she'd already mentioned spotting the herbs on their way in. For another, moving too close to the hidden burial ground might make Constant suspicious and risk jeopardizing the whole operation. Even so…

"This way," Ualan pointed south. "Just a few miles down the road. We should reach the spot by lunch."

"Lunch?" Constant growled. "I'll be out all day at this rate."

"Of course, you and I could get there much faster," Ualan looked over his shoulder as two wisps of wing-shaped light emerged from his back, "but unless you want to carry the girls all the way, we'll have to go on foot."

Constant growled, then continued plodding along toward the main road.

Christine stared in amazement at the fluttering rainbows Ualan had produced from thin air.

Nanyehi smirked. *You have no idea, kid.*

Ualan matched their gargoyle guide's slow, laborious pace, chattering away almost without taking a breath. Nanyehi was not the least bit surprised that Ualan would know exactly what topics of conversation would pique such a creature's interest.

Nanyehi and Christine moved along more briskly, and before long were far enough ahead not to risk being overheard.

"Don't go too far!" Constant called. "I don't want the girl out of my sight for a moment!"

Nanyehi turned around, waved her acknowledgment, and then brought her attention back to Christine. "I need to tell you—"

"There's something I wanted to—" Christine blurted out at almost the same moment. "Sorry." She bowed her head and turned away. "I didn't mean to—"

"No, not at all," Nanyehi assured her.

"Please, what were you going to say?"

"Oh, I'm curious now." Nanyehi playfully jabbed Christine with her elbow. "What's on your mind?"

The girl tenderly rubbed the spot Nanyehi had hit. "It's just, well, I've been having a dream lately."

Nanyehi straightened up. "Dreams can be a powerful omen."

"It's more like a memory, really," Christine said.

"Of your parents?" Nanyehi asked.

Christine nodded.

"What do they tell you?"

"Just one word. I think it might be my name."

Nanyehi stopped walking, placed a hand on Christine's shoulder, and turned to face her. "And what do they say is your name?"

The girl bit her lip. "Tayen."

Nanyehi's eyes grew wide, and her hand fell to her waist. "That's a beautiful name," she said, though perhaps more significant than either of them fully realized. She hoped the ominous feeling in the pit of her stomach didn't show on her face as they continued walking.

"Do you know what it means?"

"If I'm not mistaken, it means 'New Moon.'" It could

have been just a coincidence that this angel—paired from birth with a werewolf born under a full moon—was named after the new moon. Nanyehi didn't believe in coincidences. "Would it be alright if I called you Tayen from now on?"

The girl's brow furrowed. "I suppose I wouldn't mind; for the few hours we have left."

"That's what I wanted to talk to you about." Nanyehi could sense Tayen grow tense, her breath shallow and rapid. Was she hoping Nanyehi would spirit her away, or afraid she would? "My friend," Nanyehi turned back and nodded in Ualan's direction, a subtle hint that she was moving forward with the plan, "he has a brother about your age. His name is Moonborn."

"Moonborn? Like the curse?"

"That's right." Nanyehi gave her an impressed sideways glance.

"I learned about it in school. They say it's one of the devil's many attacks against God's children. Is his brother cursed?"

"Yes, he is," Nanyehi confirmed.

"Last night was a full moon. That poor boy…"

Nanyehi continued to be surprised at how astute this young girl truly was. "Listen, last night can be the last time he will ever transform."

Tayen's head cocked to one side as she looked up at Nanyehi. "What do you mean?"

"There's something not many people know about the curse."

"A way to break it?"

"No, just… keep it contained. You see, every werewolf has an angel. As long as the werewolf and their angel are touching during the full moon, the werewolf won't transform."

"I'm Moonborn's angel, aren't I? That's why you want to take me away from the school." If she had been hiding it before, the fear in her voice was evident now.

Nanyehi pursed her lips. "You're the only one who can help him, Tayen."

"My name's not Tayen, it's Christine!" The girl turned on her heels and bolted back toward Constant.

Nanyehi and Ualan locked eyes for a brief moment. It was now or never. Their timing would have to be perfect.

"Constant! Help!" the girl yelled.

"What's going on?" the gargoyle gurgled.

Nanyehi kept pace just behind the girl.

Ualan ran ahead of the lumbering Constant, blocking his view of the girl as his wings emerged.

Nanyehi covered her eyes. There was a blinding flash of light, and Nanyehi grabbed the girl. She clamped a hand over the child's mouth and pulled her into the dense brush on the side of the road.

Ualan took off into the air, and the dazed Constant took the bait.

He unfurled his heavy wings, and with a gust of wind and swirl of dust, he followed Ualan into the sky. "Hey! You bring her back!"

Nanyehi held Tayen tight as the girl kicked and squirmed, her screams muffled by Nanyehi's strong hand.

It would only be a matter of time before Constant realized he'd been duped, but by then it would be too late.

Nanyehi and Tayen would be long gone.

It was the only way.

# Epilogue

"It's time," the woman said over her shoulder—the same woman who had taken her from her home.

Tayen didn't look up from the doll in her lap as she delicately mended a tear in its dress. She didn't like the name 'Tayen', it didn't feel like it belonged to her. It was what these people called her, and she belonged to them now, so it would have to be her name.

"You can play with your doll later," Nanyehi insisted. "The moon will be rising soon."

Tayen had only one job to do while she lived here, only one night a month. Other than that, she was free to do as she pleased, as they had promised. She would never be asked to work on the farm, in the kitchen, or anywhere else if she didn't want to. It wasn't a bad trade, all things considered. Even so, she wanted to cling to her freedom for as long as possible.

She heard Nanyehi take a step toward her as she pulled

tight the last stitch. She snipped the thread, placed the doll on the table in front of her, then stood and turned toward Nanyehi. "I'm ready."

Nanyehi sighed and pursed her lips. "Alright, let's go."

Tayen didn't look up to meet her gaze. She didn't want to see the pity in Nanyehi's eyes.

Nanyehi led her down the hall to the cursed boy's room. Moonborn, the werewolf. The boy they all claimed Tayen had been heaven-sent to save.

Tayen winced as she entered the room. The smell was pungent; the walls bore deep gashes filled with dried blood and matted fur.

Moonborn sat at the edge of his bed, nervously glancing between Tayen and the curtained window at the far side of the room.

"Go on," Nanyehi said as she retrieved a length of rope from a side table. "Sit down."

Tayen sat on the bed next to Moonborn.

Nanyehi stepped in front of them. "You have to hold hands. There can't be any risk of your skin breaking contact."

Tayen shifted her arm so that the back of her hand rested against Moonborn's.

Nanyehi sighed as she grabbed their hands, twisted them around, and locked their fingers together.

Tayen glared at Nanyehi but didn't resist.

Moonborn glanced at the floor as his grip tightened.

Nanyehi tied the rope around their wrists, then retreated to a chair in the corner of the room next to a waiting Ualan. She took his hand, and they tied their wrists together, just the same as Tayen and Moonborn.

"Thank you." Moonborn's jaw quivered as he spoke. "I

just hope…" he glanced toward Nanyehi.

Tayen followed his gaze to where Nanyehi's hand rested on her holster. The gun was loaded with a silver bullet, she had explained earlier, just to be safe.

"Do you think it will work?" Moonborn asked.

No one felt compelled to answer. The group sat in deadly silence, interrupted only by the occasional groan of the settling farmhouse.

"I want to—" Moonborn looked at Tayen, "Can we look out the window?"

Tayen slid off the edge of the bed onto the floor and waited for Moonborn to follow. They stepped together to the window, and the floorboards creaked as Nanyehi shifted in her chair.

Moonborn reached up and pulled back the curtain.

In the corner of her eye, Tayen could see a glint of moonlight run down Moonborn's face, reflected in a single tear.

"I've never seen the full moon before," he whispered.

The story continues in…

Moonborn's Angel

Find out more at:
www.robbieballew.com